The Pinkerton Man

By the same author

Grand Valley Feud
The Beckoning Noose
Escape to Purgatory
The Early Lynching
Renegade Rose
Man Without a Yesterday
Trail to Redemption
Comanchero Rendezvous

The Pinkerton Man

MARK BANNERMAN

A Black Horse Western

ROBERT HALE · LONDON

© Anthony Lewing 2000
First published in Great Britain 2000

ISBN 0 7090 6754 2

Robert Hale Limited
Clerkenwell House
Clerkenwell Green
London EC1R 0HT

The right of Anthony Lewing
to be identified as author of this work has been
asserted by him in accordance with the Copyright,
Designs and Patents Act 1988.

Typeset by
Derek Doyle & Associates, Liverpool.
Printed and bound in Great Britain by
The Cromwell Press

*In memory of my beloved canine pal Jim,
whose passing has left me bereft.*

**With thanks to Edward Abbey and his wonderful
knowledge of the Arches Wilderness Southeast Utah**

ONE

21 June 1903. It was the day after my thirtieth birthday. It was also the day I killed a man for the first time. It gives me no feeling of pride, because I know that even outlaws have mothers, lovers, wives and children, and no heart is all black, no matter how evil. Furthermore, the killing sparked off a chain of events which twisted my fate to nigh unendurable extremes.

Today, they have erected a stone marking the spot where it all happened, in the Uinta Mountains, Utah. The stone bears the inscription: THIS IS THE SITE OF THE GUNFIGHT BETWEEN US LAW OFFICERS AND THE CHILDEATER GANG

It goes on to give brief details of the fight, but I'd rather tell you about it in my own words so you'll know exactly how it was and what followed.

In 1899, I'd returned from Cuba where I'd served as one of Teddy Roosevelt's Rough Riders, and been with him in the bloody charge near San Juan Hill. Later, when Roosevelt was in the White House, I'd taken up employment with William and Robert

Pinkerton's detective agency as an operative, just as my father had been before me. For some months I'd been tracking the Childeater gang who had left a trail of havoc behind them in the form of murder, plundered banks, trains, horse theft and general mayhem. The gang took its name from its leader, an outlaw known as Zackery 'Childeater' Hawkes. Rumour had it that he had once been part of a wagon train trapped in Rocky Mountain snows. The folk in the train had been reduced to starvation and had resorted to cannibalism. In order to survive, Zackery Hawkes was said to have killed and eaten the two children of the wagon master, but whether that's true or not I couldn't say though it would seem to fit his character. Anyway, Hawkes was dubbed 'Childeater' and, in the later years, his gang also assumed that name.

Just when I figured their trail was running cold, I crossed into Box Elder County and rode into the small town of Mule Hollow which lay on the west side of the Great Salt Lake. To my interest, I discovered that some of the Childeater outlaws had had girlfriends in this town.

The most imposing building in town was the mortician's parlour, its large lettering proclaiming UNDERTAKING – NEWEST METHODS. I wondered how 'new' methods could get. Maybe one day they'd discover how to restore life to corpses.

Nobody took much notice of me. Most of the menfolk were busy placing bets on a rooster fight at the end of the street. At the post office I learned that a couple of letters awaited collection for Nate Kirby, which I happened to know was an alias used by Zackery 'Childeater' Hawkes. This was the first big break I'd had since I'd been assigned the case, so I stuck around for a whole week, making camp in the rocks above the town, enjoying the sole companionship of my horse Jack, a gelded dun that was insignificant enough not to solicit attention – and keeping watch on the post office through my binoculars. Sometimes, I glanced at the Wanted notice of Zackery 'Childeater' Hawkes which I kept in my pocket. There was a head and shoulder portrait of him, and his darkly bearded, swarthy face and bullish neck had haunted my dreams of late. He reminded me of a hungry wolf. Years before, a piece of buckshot had injured the sclera of his right eye, leaving a permanent blood spot against the white, and this was fully displayed when he widened his eyes with anger. It was said that once you saw that spot you were as good as dead.

Seeking to banish his wild features from my mind, at least for a brief spell, I turned my attention to the local fauna, once seeing a couple of gopher snakes engaged in the ritual dance of mating. They glided side by side, as if one was the mirror image of the other, and it occurred to me that if a snake could find a compatible partner in life, why the hell hadn't I stumbled across the right woman. Too busy chasing criminals, I guessed.

On the seventh day, I saw a bosomy, straw-haired girl, obviously pregnant, pick up some mail, and ten minutes after her departure, when I checked with the postmaster, I discovered it was the Kirby mail she had taken. She had left by the west side of town, riding side-saddle on a chestnut mare, a big floppy straw hat protecting her head from the sun.

Through the alkaline dust, it was the easiest thing in the world to pick up her tracks. The trail led me well away from town, through clumps of brush and scattered junipers, into a maize of narrow ravines and weird humps of pale rock that looked like Stone Age hobgoblins. These gradually merged to form the foothills of the Uintas. As I rode, assorted creatures scuttled away ahead of me – a mule deer, kangaroo mice, a ring-tail cat, a jack rabbit; and sometimes, as I crested a ridge, I glimpsed the girl. She was in no hurry, often resting her mare, and several times she looked back, but I made sure she didn't see me. I stuck on her trail for maybe a couple of hours, the Utah sun blasting down on to the weird terrain. The girl seemed firmly set upon the route she was taking, although it struck me that this was a mighty hard horse-ride for a pregnant lady, particularly in the heat. Just as I was figuring that she would never stop, she dipped out of sight, and, following up, I saw that she was crossing over a dried-up arroyo, its gravel-covered bottom about twenty feet wide. On the far side, she drew rein and slipped from her saddle. She led her mare up a steep escarpment and both of them disappeared through the black hole of a cave entrance.

My heart started to race. It seemed that the young lady was making her mail delivery. It also seemed that I'd found what I'd been seeking. Putting two and two together, I figured I'd seen enough. I swung Jack around and heeled him back along the way we'd come. When I eventually reached Mule Hollow I telegraphed the County Sheriff at Shoshone Falls:

BELIEVE I HAVE LOCATED THE HIDEAWAY OF THE CHILDEATER GANG. SUGGEST YOU BRING AN IMMEDIATE POSSE TO EFFECT ARRESTS. WILL WAIT YOUR ARRIVAL IN MULE HOLLOW.
SIGNED: FRANK GLENGARY, PINKERTON AGENT.

In order to draw as little notice from the townsfolk as possible, I returned to my camp in the rocks; thereafter, I spent an impatient night, watching the moon come to float along the ridge above me and clouds race like clipperships across the starry sky. Presently I saw coyotes slink down, like furtive ghosts, to the outskirts of town and scavenge amongst the garbage.

I wondered if Sheriff Ollerton and his posse were already on their way. I sure hoped my conclusion that the gang was holed up in the cave was correct. Maybe I should've made doubly sure before I left the place, but there was always the chance that I might have been observed, so it was probably best this way.

Ollerton was a reliable law officer. He and eight deputies arrived at 11 o'clock next morning. Through my binoculars, I watched them ride into town and draw rein outside the Golden Goose. By the time they had stepped inside, I was on my way down to meet them. They were posing as ranchhands seeking work, but they still looked like lawmen to me, so we didn't linger, fearing that news of their arrival might somehow reach the outlaws. Soon, I was leading them along the trail I'd followed the previous day, and all the while I was praying that our quarry hadn't taken flight. I was glad Ollerton and his men were well-armed because it was sure-fire certain that the gang wouldn't give up without a fight – *if* they were still around.

Ollerton was in his fifties, a paunchy, cheerful fellow, a natural optimist, with a big, cookie-duster moustache. He was immensely proud of his new false teeth which only slipped when he laughed. Right now the excitement was showing in his florid face. 'How come you look so doggone miserable?' he enquired of me.

I discarded the stub of the cigarette I'd been drawing on. 'I don't like counting my chickens till they're hatched,' I said.

As we approached the vicinity of the cave, Ollerton split his force, sending three men in a circular movement so they could take up position on the alluvium ridges overlooking the cave entrance on the far side of the arroyo and cut off the gang's line of retreat. Meanwhile, we left our horses tethered to some shrub and crept in closer, keeping an eye open for any look-out. But everything seemed graveyard quiet, and the black opening of the cave gazed at us like an unblinking eye.

'Maybe there's a back entrance to that cave,' I whispered. 'Could be they've hightailed away.'

Ollerton shook his head. 'I don't think so. I got an itchy feeling in my bones, they're in there.'

A minute later, as if in support of his bones, a fellow appeared in the cave entrance. His clothing seemed more akin to the early part of the last century than present day. Apart from his grimy-white shirt, everything was dusty black: his Puritan hat, shapeless coat, baggy pants, boots. His beard was unkempt, shaggy and forked, but his upper lip was clean-shaven. He was scratching and stretching himself as if he'd just crawled from his bed-roll. He cupped his hands to his mouth and unleashed a loud whistle. This brought a small white dog scurrying out of the shrub lower down the arroyo. Tail a-wag, the animal trotted to his master's heel and the two of them retired into the cave.

'Who was that?' Ollerton enquired.

'Kaspar van Bremer,' I said. 'One of the van Bremer twins and Zackery Hawkes' right-hand man.'

'How come he's dressed in that funny garb?' he asked.

'Comes from a family that's tied up in a religious sect – the Hannas.' I'd made a point of studying the personalities in this case. There was a file on every known criminal at Pinkerton headquarters. 'Seems like they have their roots in the Dark Ages.'

'Well,' the sheriff commented, 'their religion must favour evil ways, that's if the van Bremers are anything to go by. Must be handy having a religion that doesn't threaten fire and brimstone every time you commit sin.' He grinned and drew his revolver. 'Anyway, seems your hunch paid off, Frank boy. One thing's certain: Never keep a dog if you want a low profile. Folks pay more attention to dogs than they do to humans.' He turned to his five men who were crouched down between some boulders and we spent a moment drawing up our plan, keeping our voices to a whisper so anybody hidden in the cave wouldn't be alerted. With a plan formulated, we checked our weapons, and I said a silent prayer that things wouldn't turn nasty. Unfortunately, God didn't hear me.

Creeping forward, we climbed down towards the arroyo, our feet making an unhealthy racket on the gravel. We reached a line of boulders. Ollerton peered over these and in his loudest voice called out, 'We know you're in there. Come out with your hands raised and nobody'll get hurt.' And he turned to me and whispered, 'Not until they slip a noose around your neck!'

Ollerton's shouted message brought a sudden response, but not in the way we'd hoped. A murderous volley of gunfire thundered from the cave, setting bullets ricocheting around our ears, sending slivers of rock slicing through the air. Lennie Crawford, a young deputy, let out a great sigh and collapsed against a boulder, and when I glanced across, a spasm shuddered through his body, setting him sliding downward into a lifeless heap, his blood soaking into the gravel.

The rest of us had ducked mighty low, hoping that the ricocheting lead and rock chippings would nestle elsewhere. If van Bremer had been remiss in whistling up the dog, at least the gang must have been well prepared for a visit such as ours. The gunfire continued for maybe two or three minutes, but it seemed much longer. As it eased, Ollerton gave me a glance, the cheerfulness drained from his face, then he nodded towards the left. A shift in position would give us a fresh perspective. Keeping our heads down, we crawled past poor Lennie Crawford and I couldn't help but pity Ollerton when it came to telling the boy's ma what had happened.

Once we took up our new position, we were better placed to commence our retaliation. We opened up with our rifles in a barrage similar to that inflicted upon us a few minutes earlier. We riddled the cave opening with bullets, but we had no indication as to whether we'd hit anybody or whether our quarry had retreated into the shelter of the depths.

When we ceased our fusillade everything fell silent, apart from the buzz of flies which were taking a busy interest in Crawford's corpse.

Ollerton was angry now, his face flushed. He licked his lips and said, 'Time we went a-visiting, boys.'

We all knew this was dangerous work, crossing the arroyo, but we climbed to our feet and nervously stepped out from behind our cover, keeping our eyes on the cave, wishing the gravel would stop crunching beneath our boots. Any moment we expected to be scythed down by bullets, but all that troubled us as we went forward was the sun's scorching heat on our necks. Guns at the ready, we climbed the slope and reached the cave entrance. What we found was nothing, apart from the inhospitable blackness of the interior. My heart was pumping right then, my whole body moist with fear. We inched our way inside, the light growing more gloomy, our boots clinking against spent shell cases. We spaced ourselves well apart so that if one of us was gunned down, the whole lot wouldn't go at the same time. At least that's what we hoped. But as the seconds passed, there was no indication that our enemies were still around. The light was now virtually non-existent and Ollerton struck a match, its scrape sounding eerily loud. As our eyes adjusted to its flickering light, we could see we were in a sizeable chamber and scattered about were blankets, cans, bottles, cigarette stubs, cooking pots and newspapers. The place had obviously been a campsite. It had also been the refuge of animals, for there were the droppings of jack rabbits and coyotes.

Ollerton swore as the match scorched his fingers and the flame gave out. Seconds later, gunfire sounded from ahead of us. Deputy Phillips said, 'Looks like there's another exit further along, and that our boys have caught them as they tried to escape.'

Ollerton grunted his agreement. 'We best be careful they don't back-track this way. Let's push on.'

And so we groped our way forward along a narrowing gallery, our senses on knife-edge, our fingers poised on our triggers. Once I cracked my head against the rock, my Stetson doing little to shield the impact. My thoughts dazedly dwelt on the prospect of a fractured skull, but then the pain diminished. Reaching up, I felt a bump rising above my temple but I figured I'd survive – at least from this blow. We crept on. The cave was an ideal hideaway. The outlaws could no doubt have hidden here for ever, had I not trailed that girl as she'd delivered the mail.

With the glimmer of light showing from ahead, we realized we were approaching the back exit. The sporadic crack of gunfire still sounded. Coming round a sort of rock outcrop, we discovered the backs of men who were directing fire out of the cave – and we immediately raised our own weapons and opened up, filling the gallery with spiteful echo. The men ahead twisted back, blasting off their own guns, and for a second I glimpsed the wolfish face of Childeater Hawkes himself. While we dodged this way and that, they charged away from us, leaving through the back exit of the cave, facing the bullets of Ollerton's men who were positioned outside. The exchange was fierce but it was brief. For maybe a couple of minutes the crack of gunfire was paramount, the air filled with spiteful lead. Then everything went quiet, apart from the awful moans of a wounded man outside the cave.

After a while, we heard our men shouting to each other from outside, though from within the cave we couldn't determine what they were actually saying. Ollerton figured it was time to make a move, so we edged forward along the gloomy gallery, wondering what carnage awaited us. Once we were within yards of the opening, Ollerton called to his three men outside, letting them know we were shortly to appear. The call came back that it was OK, but we should be mighty careful. That was something we didn't need reminding about.

We climbed out through the opening and as our eyes adjusted to the bright sunlight, we saw we were on a rock-strewn slope that was streaked with the purple of locoweed. Down to the left, a fellow was lying on his back, his groaning gradually growing fainter. He looked pretty badly hit. Across a sort of gully, our men were standing up, their rifles at the ready. Ollerton exchanged waves with them, then we started to clamber across. As we went we saw more bodies – maybe five or six. Being as dead as mutton, their limbs at grotesque angles, they didn't make attractive viewing.

'We got most of 'em,' Deputy Goodyard explained as we joined him, 'but three got away on foot, Hawkes included; nothing we could do to stop 'em. They must've had some horses hidden up in the trees.'

Ollerton cursed, then said, 'Well, we best get the bodies gathered in. I guess the world'll be a better place without them. Wish we could've got the lot.'

'Good idea o' yours to send us round the back, Sheriff,' Goodyard nodded.

That wounded outlaw was still groaning over on the far slope. It was the most mournful sound imaginable. I scrambled across to where he was sprawled. I went warily, but it didn't take much time to realize he wasn't going to pose a threat. I recognized him. He was Linus Horne and the law had been after him for years. He was wearing a sort of baseball hat with a peak. The front of his shirt was sodden with blood and there was the look of death in his eyes. He was desperate for water, but my canteen was back at my horse and I doubted he would survive long enough for me to fetch it.

'Hawkes got away,' he gasped. 'I guess . . . you'll never catch him.'

'We'll do our best,' I said, 'now you'd best get some rest.'

He nodded. The tip of his tongue flicked quiveringly across his lips, then his eyes closed, his breathing ceased and he was getting all the rest he needed.

As I rose from him, I glanced up and saw a man crouched like a black crow against a boulder way over to the left. It was clear he hadn't seen me. He was wearing that old-fashioned garb and I realized it was Kaspar van Bremer whose ill-fated dog-whistling had been the opening scene in this bloodbath. He was lifting a rifle into his shoulder, taking aim at Sheriff Ollerton as he worked lining up corpses.

In haste I raised my Army Colt and, with hardly an aim, blasted off in his direction. Six-shooters have never been renowned for accuracy, particularly at this range of some twenty yards. But my shot took him in the back of the head, bursting it open like a blood-orange, sending him tumbling forward down the slope, his rifle clattering before him. It was the luckiest shot of my life, or maybe the unluckiest; it depended which way you looked at it.

Sheriff Ollerton certainly thought it was lucky because he bought me a drink back in town that night.

I'll never forget the sight of those dead outlaws, once we had their bodies lined up. On one or two you couldn't even see the bullet holes, but most of them were shot up pretty bad; one of them for some crazy reason was smiling, or maybe he was grimacing with agony – who can tell? Lying in a neat line, their arms crossed over, divested of all weaponry, they looked quite a peace-abiding crowd, and you'd never have guessed they'd inflicted such thuggery on the community. In their pockets we found thick wads of dollar bills. Ollerton grunted with satisfaction. 'Must be the loot from the bank they robbed in Salt Lake City.'

I nodded, seeing how one wad of bills had taken the brunt of a bullet and was sodden and crimson. The money hadn't done the outlaw any good because the shell had ploughed on into his heart. In the coat pocket of another man, Deputy Goodyard discovered a small gilt-framed photograph of a young woman holding a baby. She looked truly beautiful in the sepia tint.

Goodyard remarked, 'Sure figure this no-good individual don't deserve a pretty woman like that waiting at home for him.'

I nodded, feeling downright uneasy if we'd deprived this woman of her man and the babe of its pa. 'Maybe he stole it from some poor fella he shot in the back,' I said, and this thought somehow gave me solace.

Once we'd identified the dead men to the best of our ability, Ollerton listed their names in his notebook. Then we all sat down and counted those dollar bills, some of them sticky with blood. When we reached a total, Ollerton jotted it down in his book and the money was stowed away.

Our horses were brought up and we wrapped the corpses in our sougans and set about tying them across the backs of the animals. They acted really spooked, having the equine dislike of anything deceased. As Goodyard and me were lifting the dead weight of Kaspar van Bremer, I felt something nudging my boot and realized it was van Bremer's small white dog. He looked downright forlorn. For an outlaw dog he seemed uncommonly friendly. I patted his head, and when we started back for town half an hour later, he followed along, whimpering occasionally. I guessed he was already missing his master, and thereafter he kind of hitched himself to me.

The general impression at the saloon that evening was that we'd done a satisfactory day's work, having consigned most of the Childeater gang to the town morgue. I guessed the undertaker was putting those latest methods to work right now.

There were a couple of things that distressed me. Firstly, was the death of the young deputy Lennie Crawford, who had been the apple of his mother's eye. And secondly, was the fact that at least three outlaws had got away . . . Childeater Hawkes, and two of his cohorts – one of them, I suspected, being the surviving van Bremer twin who was bound to be harbouring a blood-hatred for the man who had killed his brother Kaspar.

TWO

After the fight at the Utah cave, I went home to my father's farm in Bluegrass Kentucky, south of Frankfort, intending to rest up for a while. I kept a wary eye open in case anybody came looking for me with a gun. Pinkerton men have a knack of making enemies. Dad and I spent several peaceful evenings, sitting on the porch, watching the fireflies and listening to the crickets sing. We smoked, sipped beer, and most of the time that small dog was curled up at my feet. I'd become quite attached to him. I dubbed him 'Snowy' on account of his white coat.

Dad was slowing up, his joints swollen with rheumatism, looking his advancing years, still missing Mum who'd died five years since. He talked over the old days, just as he'd done a hundred times before, relating how he'd started out as a detective with the Pinkertons when they'd first commenced business. 'Got a reference from George Custer,' he'd said as if I hadn't known, 'and on the strength of that, Pinkerton employed me. Pinkerton was a fine man. He uncovered a plot to kill Abe Lincoln soon after he was elected to the presidency. Pity he wasn't on hand to stop John Wilkes Booth assassinating him five years later.' And then Dad would go on about how he, himself, had brought peace to the West virtually single-handed until his health had eventually cracked under the strain. 'Private detectives was what this country needed, Frank boy, because they could cross jurisdictional borders, otherwise we'd never have whipped the Molly Maguires, or the Daltons or Youngers.'

According to Dad, after he retired things went downhill. But he'd been pleased when I'd joined the Pinkertons and now he smiled proudly when I told him how the Childeater gang had been smashed. Pity, though, that Childeater himself had escaped the net.

I wasn't allowed respite for long because a telegraph message arrived at the farm from Robert Pinkerton. My orders were succinct:

TRACK DOWN AND ARREST JASON VAN BREMER.

Since I'd killed his twin brother, I'd figured that it might be Jason who would do the tracking . . . of me! Now the boot was on the other foot. But one thing seemed certain. When we met up, there wouldn't be many pleasantries exchanged.

I'd heard that the van Bremer boys had been born and raised in the Arches country of south-east Utah. The father ran some sort of smallholding way out in the wilds, bringing up his family in the strong religious code that he'd adopted. Like Sheriff Ollerton had said, it seemed real strange that a religious family should have produced a couple of ne'er-do-well outlaws as sons – but maybe there was more to it than met the eye. Both Dad and I reckoned that if I was to track down Jason van Bremer, then the best place for starting the search was at the family residence, though, in truth, it was unlikely that he would show up around there once he knew the law was on his tail. But at least I might get some clue as to his whereabouts.

So I bade farewell to Dad, seeing a tear in his eye. I shook his hand, feeling the frailty in him, and hoped we'd both survive to enjoy another reunion. As I nudged Jack away, with the dog trotting along behind, I little realized the nightmare I was headed for.

Within a week, I was paying my first visit to south-east Utah, a seemingly endless succession of lava-capped mesas, canyons, red cliffs and and tablelands. Eventually I came upon the township of God's Navel nestled in a valley. The place had one wide street, lined with two saloons and numerous brick stores some of which boasted balconies. I noticed how one store offered wallpaper, stationery, crayons, beauty creams and stereoscopic views. I figured I'd get some of those views for my stereoscope, which I'd left with Dad. The most impressive building in town was a branch of the Goldwater Bank.

A few enquiries set me on the lonesome ride towards the van Bremer homestead.

If I'd thought the previous terrain I'd crossed was

weird, then what I now encountered was like another planet. The trail wound past numerous natural rock arches, windows in stone, holes in the rock. Every one was different. Some were just big enough for a man to crawl through, while others were so high you could've built a cathedral under them. Many resembled jug handles or flying buttresses and were topped by natural pinnacles and minarets, everything designed courtesy of the erosion of wind and water during the last few million years or so. I guessed it had once been the bed of some prehistoric ocean. Now the colouring of the terrain, pink, brown and red, changed as the sun radiated a final explosive blaze and dissolved into its westward drift. I felt dwarfed by it all, my shadow lost amid far greater shadows, and the clop of Jack's hooves sounded intrusively loud.

Three hours after leaving God's Navel, I got my first glimpse of the homestead. With the brittle heat giving way to softening coolness of dusk, I pulled up at the fringe of ragged piñon pine, and gazed down into the valley below. Lantern glow glinted from the cabin's windows. The place stood on the slope flanking a watercourse, a zigzag creek with a long low bluff on its far bank. It was a single-storey, sprawling cabin with a porch and a lean-to kitchen at the side. It was built of rock and slate, and smoke was coming from its main chimney. There were several cedarwood outhouses, including a barn and a granary, and they all had strange white hex signs daubed on their walls. A corral was at the side containing about six horses – all blacks except for one piebald. I can't explain why, but the sight of those animals somehow gave me the feeling that my quarry was closer at hand than I'd dared hope.

There was a echoey feeling in this valley, like it somehow belonged to another age, and that was emphasized by the cabin which gave the impression it had stood there since colonial days. Along the slope, a wheatfield had been cultivated. Another area was fenced with juniper posts and wire, no doubt to confine cows which had now been driven into a barn for the night.

When I saw a fellow moving out to fasten the shutters and drive the hogs back into their pen, I guessed this was old man van Bremer, the widowered father of the outlaw twins, and gazing through my binoculars I could see the bygone style of his dress, broad-brimmed black hat, black coat, and baggy pants. I reckoned it was crazy walking around like that in this modern twentieth century, but he was no doubt governed by the customs of the religion he'd adopted. Each man to his own, I thought, but how on earth had he come to sire a couple of black-as-sin outlaws? Maybe they'd rebelled against his sanctimonious ways. He was a thick-set man with a bullishness about the way he moved, and there was a dog of similar build following him around. I wondered if back in the cabin, his surviving son was forted up; and if the old man was aware that Kaspar had been shot. Maybe he even knew who'd done the shooting.

As I overlooked the homestead from a shadowy piñon pine, I saw the woman join him. She was wearing a white bonnet and a long black dress with a shawl over her shoulders. She busied herself shooing chickens back into their coop, making sure it was secure with a large bolt, shutting everything down for the night. Backing it all, I could hear a sound like the cooing of pigeons. It puzzled me, but suddenly I noticed something else and my puzzlement changed to gut-sinking shock.

There wasn't just one dog down there, but two. The second looking downright familiar. When I glanced around, I discovered that Snowy had left me and descended to the homestead – the first time he'd left my heel since I'd inherited him – and I cursed my stupidity. I should have realized that the animal had 'come home'. Right now, he was exchanging a tail-wagging greeting with the other dog, and both man and woman were clearly surprised at his arrival, even glancing upslope at the trees where I was ducking down.

The words of Sheriff Ollerton came to haunt me: *Never keep a dog if you want a low profile.*

I gave Snowy another name, one he maybe didn't deserve. But those folks down at the cabin would now have a sure-fire indication that something odd was afoot. They went back inside, and perhaps there they were conferring with Jason and putting two and two together.

I tried to draw up a plan.

With night coming in, embracing everything with a dense stillness, it seemed pointless playing my hand right now. Better to let them stew over things for the night, and go in at dawn and arrest Jason van Bremer, when they were all bleary-eyed.

The Pinkerton Man

I'd hobbled Jack a long way back in the trees. The grazing there was adequate, just about, and I didn't want him getting scent of those horses down in the corral. He was gelded but wouldn't be averse to setting up a long-range conversation.

I figured that when the moon came out, the cabin would be reasonably illuminated and it would be as well to maintain a watch on it, making sure Jason van Bremer didn't attempt to escape. To keep myself awake and vigilant, I unsheathed my weapons and set about cleaning them. I didn't want any blockages or misfires when I had the outlaw in my sights. I figured an accurate shot or two in his legs would be sufficient to bring him down. I could then make my arrest and take him back to civilization to stand trial. I didn't fancy another killing if I could help it. I'd leave that to justice and the rope to deal with.

Despite my distaste of sudden death, I'd been associated with guns for most of my life, my dad having placed much emphasis on the development of my weaponry skills. I'd always adopted the attitude that a well-armed man was liable to attract more respect than a fellow who walked around with just a penknife in his pocket. In consequence, I now sat cross-legged in the moonlight above the cabin, and with rag and oil set about cleaning my Army Colt revolver and my magazine-loading rifle. I'd started on the latter when the craziest thing imaginable happened. I can't offer any plausible excuse apart from over-confidence and rank banality.

Still wondering what was happening down at the cabin, I was about to unload the chamber of the rifle when the weapon seemed to explode in my hands. Maybe a faulty round stuck in the breech. The unexpected detonation was deafening and somehow drove the bolt back with bullet-like force into my right hand between thumb and forefinger. I guess I yelled out with shock, but the strange thing was that there wasn't any immediate pain, not physical anyway. When I glanced at what had happened, I felt like throwing up. The metal bolt was sticking out of my hand like an extra finger, its base deeply embedded in the webbed flesh that separated thumb from fingers. My thumb seemed to be dangling by no more than a thread of skin, and already blood was welling out at an alarming rate.

For a moment, I could do nothing more than slump there, stunned and crying out with anguish at what had happened. I felt sick, dizzy, faint and suddenly the pain registered. Pain ... my God, I'd never known anything like it! White, shattering torture throbbed up my arm from the extremity of what was left of my hand.

Somehow, I pulled the bolt away from my hand, ripped my bandanna from my throat and drew it tight about the pumping blood. I felt light-headed. I was losing consciousness, but I was brought back to full awareness by the sound of dogs baying, a man's shouts, and glancing down I saw that the cabin door had been thrown open and lantern light was spewing forth.

Hunched over with pain, cradling my injured hand, I forced myself up. The sound of the explosion had alarmed those in the cabin. Already suspicious

The Pinkerton Man

because of the reappearance of the dog, old man van Bremer and whoever else was down there, must be coming to investigate, even at this moment rushing up the slope.

There's no point in prevaricating: I was weeping with the agony, mindful that the blood was turning my bandanna sodden. Everything seemed to be whirling about me, like a demonic nightmare, and backing it all I was aware of the dogs barking, of the shadowy figures that had emerged from the cabin, and they were surely carrying guns. I was too badly injured to put up a fight. If they found me, a quick bullet would surely seal my fate. Maybe putting me out of my suffering would be no bad thing; even so instinct had me scrambling up the slope, hoping that I might be able to reach my horse, or better still that some miracle would present itself and provide me with unforeseen sanctuary.

The slope was wooded with low piñon pine, but beneath the trees was nothing but shale made slippery by pine needles. Time and again my boots slid, and I was unable to reach out with my injured right hand and so fell, jarring myself painfully. Behind me I could hear the rush of pursuit, and if I could hear them, I was sure-fire certain they could hear me. In my panic, I'd left my own weapons behind, but, at least, beneath the pines there was shadow and even some points of concealment. But if I still cherished hope of escape, I had overlooked one thing – or rather two.

The dogs.

I blundered to the left, my breath coming like the

rasp of a sawmill. Behind me, I heard a man's wheezy cough followed by the metallic clink of a rifle being cocked.

My senses were ebbing. I fell, and was helpless to prevent myself rolling downward, sending shafts of pain through my arm, then I came to a joggling halt with my back wedged against a rock, the breath slammed from my body. I could do nothing else but roll into a protective ball, clamp my eyes shut and submit to my fate.

A dog's snarl sounded, the beast's hot breath brushing my neck. I got my eyes open, and knew that the large black canine was crowding in on me. But suddenly the animal seemed shouldered aside and Snowy's tongue sought out my face, applying a moist persistent lick, registering an affectionate greeting that was in no way compatible with my own sentiments. Nor indeed with those of the other dog; it crouched just behind Snowy, its teeth still showing white in the gloom.

However it was the dark bulk of the man that was the most intimidating. He loomed like some mediaeval master of hounds, his craggy, bearded face, bathed in the glow of the low-held lantern, the vicious clink of cold steel leaving no doubt that the slightest tightening of his finger would be sufficient to finish me.

His voice came as a sibilant hiss: '*Who art thou?*'

'I'm . . .' My brain sought some convenient lie, but failed. My senses felt like bludgeoned pulp. I gave up my battle, slipped into welcome blackness, only dimly aware of the old man's cough.

THREE

I felt I was stuck on a raft in a whirlpool, spinning around giddily, totally powerless to control my own destiny.

'Mama,' a tiny voice cried out, 'I think he's waking up.'

I sensed an additional presence and a woman said, 'I guess the sedative is wearing off.'

'He won't hurt us, will he, Mama?'

'Not in his state, he won't, Ella.'

I got my eyes open and gradually things swam into weird focus. I was lying in a bed. The room was small and barely furnished, its low ceiling beamed, its walls timber planking, lining the rock, and adorned by pictures of figures wearing halos. It seemed like night-time. The place was lit by flickering candles. On the wall I could see a large framed quotation:

Blessed are the poor in spirit: for theirs is the kingdom of heaven.

Above me the woman's face swam like a cork in a gentle swell. I guessed she was in her mid-twenties.

She looked as if she'd just stepped out of a history book. She was wearing a little bonnet of white lace and a plain gingham dress. At first I thought she, too, had a halo above her head, that she was some sort of angel descended from Heaven, but I realized my vision was playing tricks. Her eyes were dark; deep pools of concern.

'Who are you?' I gasped.

'Rebecca van Bremer,' she responded simply, and as my brain absorbed this revelation, I recalled my nightmare scramble to escape, and the terrible pain in my arm, and thinking about the pain brought it throbbing back. I groaned and tried to move.

'No point in disturbing thyself,' Rebecca van Bremer said. 'We have sent for the doctor but it may be some hours before he arrives. Thou have a terrible wound. How did it happen?'

I swallowed hard. 'My gun went off when I was cleaning it. It was crazy.' The explanation sounded so inadequate. What self-respecting fellow would shoot himself in the hand? But the woman seemed to take it all in her stride, nodding understandingly, and suddenly I recalled the purpose of my mission, and the danger I was in. 'Where's Jason . . . Jason van Bremer?' I kept my voice low in case he was listening.

'He's not here now,' she answered. 'Thou have been asleep for many hours. My father-in-law has a very strong sedative which Doctor O'Connell gave him to ease his cough and help him to sleep. We gave some to thee, after he brought thee in.'

'Your father-in-law?' I murmured.

She nodded. 'Frederik van Bremer.'

She reached forward, tidying the quilt that covered me. I saw how her hair was braided and neatly coiled around her head. Then my eye fell upon the gold band on her finger. It drew my attention as if it were a beacon.

'So you must be the wife of. . . ?' I left the question hanging, fearing the answer.

She frowned, then, dropping her voice to a husky whisper, she said, 'Kaspar.'

'But my daddy's dead,' the little girl Ella piped up. I'd almost forgotten about her, standing alongside my bed, half hidden by her mother's skirts. She was dressed in similar plain fashion to her mother but she was wearing a small apron. 'We have said prayers for him.'

'I know he's dead. I'm real sorry.' I murmured, then inwardly cursed yet another example of my stupidity. The words had slipped out before my brain could bridle my tongue.

'How come thou know about Kaspar's death?' This time it was the old man's voice, coming from the room's doorway. His spoke with a slow deliberation, a belligerence in his tone. He must have been listening all along. I glanced across and got a good look at him for the first time. He was still wearing his black hat and coat. For some strange reason it was fastened with hooks and eyes instead of buttons and buttonholes, I noticed. His shirt was rough cotton, open-necked and he had the familiar untrimmed beard, forked like a swallow's tail, with no moustache.

My mind grappled with what he had asked. Even

as I winced at the pain in my arm, I felt overwhelmingly shameful. I wanted to shout out, *I couldn't help it! I had to do it!* I had killed this man's son, this woman's husband, this little girl's daddy....

'I asked thee a question,' the old man repeated. 'How come thou knew Kaspar had gone to his Maker?' His anger was increasing. Did he already know? He was blocking the doorway. He looked uncommonly fierce and he still held his gun.

Yet again I blabbed out the first thing that came into my mind. 'I was with him when he died.'

'With him?' Rebecca van Bremer queried.

I nodded. I looked at her face in the uncertain light of the candles. Everything seemed to be turning red. I closed my eyes, hoping unconsciousness would spirit me away and I would be able to climb out of the mire I was digging myself into, but it didn't and I heard the old man cough impatiently. I raised my eyelids and gave the only explanation I could think of.

'I was a member of the gang. I was there when the law hit us up in the Uinta Mountains. I saw Kaspar shot.' And then my glance met the deep pools that were the eyes of Rebecca van Bremer, and I added, 'He died real quick. He didn't suffer, I swear it.'

She nodded her prim head.

'And who art thee?' the old man persisted.

The pain in my arm seemed to be getting worse. I realized my hand had been bandaged, but already the blood was seeping through.

'I'm Linus Horne,' I lied. It was the only name I

could think of, and for an awful moment I wondered if these people would have known the real Linus who had been shot down with the other outlaws. If so, I would be exposed as a fake.

But old Frederik seemed to relax and accept my explanation. 'Well one thing's certain, Linus Horne. Thou art not going anywhere, not in that state. Thou had best wait till the doctor gets here.'

I felt alarmed. I knew I was very badly hurt and thoughts of amputation reared in my mind. But the woman took my concern to mean something else. 'Don't worry,' she murmured. 'Dr O'Connell won't turn thee over to the law. Thou art not the first outlaw he has treated.'

A sudden thought came to me, another fear. Perhaps these people were not all they seemed; perhaps they were tricking me. 'If you, your father-in-law and little Ella are alone here at the cabin,' I said, 'who's gone to fetch the doctor?'

She hushed me by holding her finger to her lips and saying, 'Listen!'

I held my breath, straining my ears for sound, as instructed. At first, all I could hear was the heavy tick of a big clock, then something else caught my attention, something I'd heard previously. It was a low cooing sound, coming from outside the window.

'Pigeons?' I said.

She nodded. 'I have sent the pigeon, James, to Blessedville with a message for the doctor. James will not let us down.'

'Blessedville?' I queried. I had never heard of the place.

'Other folks have another name for it. But we think it is a blasphemous name, not worthy of the Lord.'

'God's Navel?' I gasped, and the old man coughed reprovingly as if mention of the town's name in his home was sinful.

'Oh . . .' I lay back. My circumstances were growing more bizarre by the minute. One thing seemed certain. Unless I got medical treatment, and fast, I was going to be even worse off.

'I shall pray for thee,' Rebecca announced. 'I shall pray that thy injury will be healed, and that thou will give up thy wicked ways.'

'I will pray too,' the little girl Ella proclaimed, and true to their word they both knelt down at my bedside, each steepling their hands, closing their eyes and the woman's words came steadfastly: 'Oh Lord, please have mercy on Linus Horne, make sure he does not bleed to death, heal his wound and make him turn away from his wicked ways so that his feet are set firmly on the path of righteousness.'

The woman had a startling, serene candidness. Later I learned that for a woman to tell a falsehood could lead to excommunication from the Hanna faith. Right then I felt as low as a slug crawling through slime and this drove the realization of my own hypocrisy into me. For a brief moment my glance swung to old Frederik, standing in the doorway of the room. I had the feeling that he did not share the woman's compassion, that any prayer he was mouthing would have me suffering a far less pleasant fate.

A sudden thought struck me. 'My horse. He's hobbled up there in the trees.'

Rebecca nodded understandingly. 'We'll get him brought in.'

I closed my eyes, allowed recollection of Rebecca's soothing prayer to fill my mind and lull me into sleep, to temporarily blind me to the awesome possibilities that hovered over me once these folks found out who I really was and, even worse, discovered what I had done.

It seemed hours later. The shutters had been thrown back and sunlight was streaming through the cabin windows. I realized that Ella was in the room, watching me.

As she saw me stir she turned and rushed out, calling, 'Mama, he's awake. Linus is awake and he looks real hungry.'

A moment later, Rebecca appeared in the doorway. She was carrying my six-shooter and rifle, holding them with disdainful fingertips, as if they were instruments of the devil. 'Father-in-law brought thy horse in, and he also found these weapons.' She placed the guns on the table across the room. I noticed how all the ammunition had been stripped from the belt. 'He took the bullets away,' she added, 'in case thou did thyself any more harm.'

I nodded and thought *and in case I try to escape from here*.

She disappeared and soon I heard the clink of pans and then the sizzle of frying pork. Its flavoursome aroma had me licking my lips, made me realize how ravenous I was.

She returned with the tray, placed it on the dresser next to the bed. 'Thou had better eat, keep up thy strength.'

The pork was in wide strips, mostly lean with only little streaks of fat interlarding it. In addition there was crusty bread, cheese and a cup of creamy milk.

'After thou have eaten that,' she said, 'I will bring thee some shoofly pie.'

'I'm grateful,' I said.

I was about to start eating, when little Ella appeared at my bedside and said, 'Don't thou say grace?'

'Oh yes,' I said, feeling reprimanded, then I started, 'For what we are about to receive . . .' But again I was interrupted.

'We always say grace in silence,' Ella said.

1 nodded and moved my lips in silent prayer. When that was done I was allowed to eat.

The meal was wholesome and I wiped my plate clean with the bread. Then Rebecca brought me a piece of her shoofly pie. Scarcely had I finished, when I heard Frederik call from outside. 'There is somebody coming. It could be Jason!'

I straightened up with a jolt, wincing at the pain it caused. I know that Jason would surely recognize me as the one who had killed his twin, that all the kindness I had been shown, in the belief that I was his confederate, would be blown sky high. For a moment wild ideas of leaping up and escaping from this place crowded in on me ... but then Frederik's voice sounded again. 'No. It is not Jason. It is the doctor.'

I looked at the blood-spotted dressing that enveloped my hand. My immediate fear of Jason's return was replaced with concern as to what the doctor's prognosis would be.

FOUR

I suspected the only reason the van Bremers had shown mercy was because they had accepted my story that I belonged to the Childeater gang, and at this stage there seemed no point in revealing my real identity. Certainly in my present state, being half-drugged with the old man's cough mixture, and crippled with the spreading pain from my arm, I was in no condition to run off.

I heard the stomping and blowing of a horse from outside, and then a brief exchange of words between Frederik and the new arrival. Within a minute, Dr O'Connell was ushered in. He was trailed by all three van Bremers, little Ella's eyes as wide as saucers.

O'Connell was a barrel-chested, cumbersome-looking man in a frock coat that was too tight. He removed his hat, wiped the sweat from his brow with his coat sleeve. Rebecca brought him a mug of water and as he slurped it back, his eyes flicked over me, disdain showing on his heavy-jowled face. Even if my right hand hadn't been in the mess it was, I doubt we'd have been on hand-shaking terms. 'Treating criminals has its drawbacks,' he commented as he drained the mug. 'They tend to be unreliable paying bills.'

Old Frederik said, 'I will have no debts. I will see thy bill is paid.'

O'Connell nodded thoughtfully, then he told me to lift my arm out from beneath the quilt which I did. He grimaced at the sight of my blood-spotted bandage. I noticed how his nostrils were quivering. When he paused, he said, 'Just checking for the whiff of gangrene. I've always had an uncanny talent for sniffing it out. Gained experience during the war.'

'Do you smell gangrene?' I enquired anxiously.

'Can't tell,' he responded. 'I've got a cold. There's an epidemic of influenza sweeping town. Hope I haven't picked it up. Now then, young man, let's have that bandage off.'

He produced a small pair of scissors from his leather bag and with a surprising gentleness started to cut the soggy bandage from what was left of my hand. 'Shot yourself, eh?' he commented. 'Like I've always said, guns are like women. If you don't treat 'em right, there's no telling what they'll do. I . . . *my God!*' His eyes widened as he pulled the last layer of bandage away and got his first clear view of my hand. As for me, I didn't dare look. He sighed deeply. 'That confirms my original diagnosis. Could turn gangrenous all right.' He placed his palm on my forehead. 'You're running a fever and you've lost so much blood, it's a wonder there's any left.'

'What does that mean, Doc?' I enquired, feeling utterly sick.

He took my forearm in his thick hands, peered close, probing it with his fingers. 'Means your only option may be to have the hand lopped off, say about a couple of inches above the wrist. Wouldn't take long. I could do it at my surgery in town. I had plenty of experience in Cuba, though I might have to get some help. You mustn't leave it too long, 'less you want to lose the whole arm.'

I didn't respond. I could see Rebecca and little Ella standing behind the doctor, their faces as white as alabaster.

'You come into town,' O'Connell went on. 'Maybe tomorrow or the next day, and we'll get the job done. That's if I haven't gone down with the influenza. You can rest at my place after the surgery. May be able to fix you up with some sort of hook or even a false hand, though they don't come with flexible trigger fingers. You'll have to do your gunfighting left-handed, though maybe it'd be best if you steered clear of guns. There's no point in tempting Providence.'

I swallowed hard and tried to imagine that I was in some sort of nightmare, that I'd wake up soon and be back at my father's farm, sitting on the porch sipping cool beer. But no matter how hard I tried, the nightmare wouldn't go away.

O'Connell asked for some hot water in a bowl, and Rebecca rushed away to put the kettle on. While we waited, he took a roll of bandage from his bag. Soon he was trying unsuccessfully to restore my unhinged thumb to its rightful place while I gazed at the ceiling and bit on my lip to stop myself yelling out. Shortly, he was bathing the hand, doing his best to reduce the discomfort but not succeeding. After he'd finished, he wrapped the bandage around and fastened it with a pin. 'It'll all come off in a day or so,' he remarked, 'so there's no point in worrying too much. Try taking Frederik's sedative. It'll help you sleep.'

I nodded my thanks. I wasn't exactly overwhelmed with gratitude despite the fact that he was fully convinced about the accuracy of his words. As for me, I had other ideas. My mind was racing like a two-year-old filly.

Once the doctor departed, I was going to follow suit and escape from this place. Maybe good clean fresh air and a positive attitude would create some sort of miracle. I sure prayed so.

I must have dozed. When I came awake I could hear voices sounding from another room in the cabin. The air was redolent with the scent of juniper. Rebecca must be burning some to sweeten the air. Recollections of the doctor's visit swept up on me with depressing impact. My hand and arm felt as if somebody was pounding them with a sledgehammer. I glanced around the room. The window was wide open. Outside, I could see a line of clothes hung out to dry. I recognized my own shirt and jeans. I raised the blanket and gazed at what was beneath. I was stark naked. Rebecca must've stripped me in my drugged condition, and my cheeks were suddenly burning.

I reckoned I'd grab my clothes and then get to the

corral, hoping my horse Jack had been placed in there with the others. Maybe I had little chance of getting away, but I had to try. I knew my dad had a distinguished physician as a friend in Frankfort. Perhaps if I got back to Kentucky, he could do something for me. I was fond of my hand. I determined to keep it.

I cast back the quilt, seeing that it was made up of many patches, all joined with fancy stitching which I guessed was Rebecca's nimble work. I swung my legs over the side of the bed and lowered my feet on to the cold flagstone floor. I felt befuddled and weak, but I gritted my teeth and forced myself to stand up. That was when everything seemed to turn green, everything swirling about me like fish in deep, dark water, and my legs became jelly and I hit the floor with an awful thump, knowing that without help I hadn't got sufficient strength to get back into bed, let alone hightail away to freedom.

FIVE

It was old Frederik who heard the thump of my fall and rushed into the room. He stood over me, gazing down, and at that moment I saw in him his son Kaspar, the man I'd killed, and my insides churned.

I stammered out a lame reason for my predicament. 'I tried to turn over and fell out of bed.'

He paused for what seemed an age, then he nodded. He stooped down. 'Get thy nakedness covered, man. Put thine arm around my shoulder and I'll help thee up.'

I grunted my thanks and complied, smelling the corn tobacco on his breath, and a moment later I was back in bed with the quilt pulled over.

'Be careful,' he advised, 'else thou will do thyself even greater damage. Thou must beware of guns. Guns are the instruments of the devil, but the Lord has granted us permission to use them. We have to treat them with respect. I once knew a man who forgot he'd slipped a cleaning rod down his barrel. When he took a pot shot at a rabbit, he nigh blew his head off. I guess that rabbit must have died of laughing.' The old man chuckled and I figured he was not so fearsome as I'd at first supposed, but his next words chilled me. 'Thou do much talking in thy sleep. I have never known a man talk so much.'

'I'm sorry,' I mumbled, deeply worried. Talking in my sleep? What secrets had I revealed?

He didn't enlighten me but departed. I lay back. Effectively, I was a prisoner in this place. They could drug me and do what they chose. They could have my hands chopped off, even my legs, and I'd be unable to resist.

I don't know how long I slept for, but I was plagued by nightmares of a surgeon's knife slicing into me; the knife wasn't wielded by a doctor, but by Kaspar van Bremer and he was grinning fit to bust. I awoke with a shout. I felt a moist, cooling compress against my forehead and looked up to see Rebecca's compassionate face. She was leaning over me, the gentle pressure of her breasts touching me. It was night-time again, the room bathed in the soft glow of the candle. I gazed into her shadowy face. She had removed her bonnet and I could see how her hair was parted in the middle. I suddenly realized how beautiful she was. There was a delicate symmetry about her features, and feathery lashes framed her dark eyes. Youth still showed in the slight puffiness of her lips and the smooth flesh of her neck, and despite the drabness of her high-buttoned dress, I felt intensely aware of her body.

Would all her kindness slip away when she knew the truth? That I had inflicted widowhood upon her? I groaned.

'You must be angry with those who killed your

husband,' I said tentatively. 'You would like to see them punished?'

She frowned. 'I would wish violence on no person.'

'Not even if you came face to face with them?'

'Our faith decrees that our women will never raise their voices in anger, nor show violence.'

'Only the women?' I exclaimed. 'How about the men?'

'They are allowed to show violence when it is necessary.'

I reckoned I had probed this subject far enough. I'd gleaned some slight reassurance, though I still had plenty to worry about. I swung my thoughts to other things. I raised my blanket and inspected myself. I was no longer naked. I was wearing a nightshirt. It was incredible what folks could do to you, unbeknown, when you were drugged. That sedative was more potent than liquor.

She read my thoughts. 'The nightshirt belonged to Kaspar. He will not need it any more.' She removed the compress, felt my head with her hand. 'I think thy fever is subsiding,' she murmured. 'I think the good Lord is answering our prayers.' She remoistened the compress from a bowl and returned it to my brow. It was greatly comforting – or was it her nearness, her serenity, that somehow calmed me?

'The doctor brought the pigeon James home,' she said. 'He is a loyal bird. We sent him to tell the doctor how bad thou were hurt. Do thou remember?'

'Yes. I'm grateful to the bird. At least I think I am.'

'Dr O'Connell will do his best for thee. Despite his gruff manner, he is a good Christian, though not of our faith.' She frowned and then added, 'Another pigeon has arrived with a message from town. Apparently outlaws have held up the Goldwater Bank, wounded the teller and stolen much money. It must have been terrible. The robbers were masked.' She lowered her gaze. 'They're blaming my brother-in-law for it.'

'Jason?'

She nodded.

'Where is he now?' I asked.

She closed her eyes, shaking her head from side to side. 'He comes and goes as he pleases. I think he has a woman friend. He makes his own rules.'

'So he could come back here at any time?'

She gave me a strange look, then she said, 'Yes.' She rose, picking up the bowl. 'Now thou must rest some more, Linus. Sleep is what thou need to get the fever out of thy body.' She blew out the candle and left me in darkness.

I lay motionless. I wondered, once an amputation had taken place, if the pain would immediately lessen, or would it be even worse?

I could hear movement in the other cabin rooms. Presently came the sonance of Ella reciting her prayers before she went to sleep. It sounded through the thin wall, but I couldn't hear the words distinctly enough to know if I was included. I smiled to myself. She was a pretty child. She reminded me of a little angel, though sometimes there was an impish light in her eye. I hoped she'd grow up to be as sweet as her mother.

I needed a pee and, groping beneath the bed with

my good hand, I located the chamberpot. I knelt on the boards and raised Kaspar's nightshirt. As I finished and climbed back, I realized I had completed the feat without falling over. My legs had felt much stronger. Thoughts of another attempt at escape flitted through my mind. I was planning it when I must have drifted into sleep.

I was awakened by a loud thumping. I sat up. It was still dark. Somebody was banging on the outer door of the cabin. 'Open up!' a voice yelled. 'We're representing the law.'

There was a pause, then I heard old Frederik call out, 'Wait. I will let thee in.' And presently lantern light flared, showing through the crack in my doorway, and I heard bolts being drawn back.

I suddenly realized that Rebecca had appeared at my bedside, looking ghost-like in her white nightdress.

'I feared this,' she whispered. 'Thou must climb through the window and hide outside. Quickly!'

I slid out of bed, was stumbling towards the window when I swung back. I fumbled in the gloom and found my six-shooter on the table. Maybe old Frederik had left a bullet or two in the chamber after all.

'Quickly . . . for the Lord's sake!' Rebecca repeated, giving me a supporting push.

She unfastened the shutter from the inside, quietly eased it open, then she helped me as I swung my legs over the sill and climbed out into the moonlit night. I stumbled forward, little pieces of sharp rock stabbing at my bare feet. I was aware of booted footsteps sounding from the front porch. I glanced back but saw no sign of Rebecca through the darkened window. For a second, I felt uncertain. If it was law enforcement officers visiting the cabin, I could declare my true identity and probably be unharmed. On the other hand, if it was their intention to apprehend Jason van Bremer, they would be disappointed and might well vent their frustration on me. Furthermore, the prospect of betraying Rebecca and old Frederik made me blench. So I decided my best plan was to make myself scarce, at least for the present.

I started through the gloom, hoping that my white nightshirt wouldn't give me away. But my hopes were dashed. A gun snapped out from ahead of me, two shots, and I felt the impact of a bullet, like a white-hot wire of pain, high up on my left shoulder. It sent me staggering and, scarcely grasping what was happening, I imagined the ground rose up to hit me, driving the breath out of me. For a second I just lay there, cursing my stupidity, realizing that it should have been obvious that the visitors would position a man at the rear of the cabin to catch anybody attempting a quick getaway, using the same ploy as Sheriff Ollerton had done so effectively in the Uinta Mountains. It was the oldest trick in the world. However, all self-recrimination was terminated. Somebody was pacing towards me, their feet rustling the grass.

I was sprawled belly-flat, my injured hand crushed by the fall. But miraculously I was still gripping the pistol in my left hand. The footsteps came closer, and there was an unsteadiness about them, and with that unsteadiness came the unmistakable taint of whiskey fumes. I kept prone, but inside I was as tense as a compressed spring. My great fear was that my attacker might fire another shot into me, finish the job he had started. But instead, he hooked his boot beneath my belly, no doubt intending to flip me over to establish my identity. He didn't get the chance. I'd taken enough punishment and I was angry. I twisted over, moving with every ounce of speed my battered frame could muster. I scythed the air with the pistol, catching him a cracking blow just below the knee. He howled out with pain, doubling forward. I was on my feet in a flash, driving my knee into his undefended groin, knowing instantly that I had hit the bull's-eye. The gun had slipped from his grasp. I pistol-whipped his head with the barrel of my own gun, so desperate that I knew there could be no finesse, no fair play, in this struggle. Under my rain of blows, he collapsed, lay groaning, then he went quiet and the thought was in me that I'd killed him.

My own weapon had served me effectively, but I now discovered that old Frederik had completely emptied the chamber, and its further use was limited. Stooping in the darkness, I located my assailant's six-shooter and grabbed it.

My heart was pounding, my breath heaving, but I tried to take stock. Right now I could run off into the darkness, maybe escape from this place, get my medical problems resolved and take retirement from the Pinkerton force. But then I heard Rebecca's scream, coming from the cabin, and I remembered that my assailant had not been operating alone. Suddenly a man's voice called out, 'You all right, Jake?'

In a slurred voice, only sufficiently audible to carry, I mumbled, 'Over here . . . I got him!'

As I crouched in the darkness, I saw two men step out from the cabin's open doorway, their figures silhouetted against the interior lantern glow, their boots creaking the porch's boards. They were approaching me when I opened up, left-handed, with the six-shooter, thankful that its previous owner had left it partially charged. The two shadowy figures scattered in front of me, but now the crack of rifle fire erupted from the cabin and I guessed that old Frederik had been able to grab his rifle and was now supplementing my fire.

If these were law-officers, I had no wish to hit anybody, just to scare them off – but Frederik had no such reservations, because I heard a man curse and his gun clattered down. His companion was crying out, 'Don't shoot no more. You got us beat!' and with that I heard a scurrying movement as they ran off into the night. Shortly came the thud of departing hooves.

I remembered the man who had tried to gun me down and turned back to him. To my surprise and relief, he was clambering to his feet, half falling again in the process. I kept him covered with the gun and I saw the whites of his eyes in the gloom. 'OK, mister, you win,' he grunted out. 'I don't know who the hell you are, but we won't trouble you no more.'

'Get out of here!' I shouted. 'Don't come back!'

He gave me what must have been a hateful scowl, then he turned and staggered off into the darkness. One thing was certain. If he didn't find his horse out there, he was going to have a long walk back to town – or wherever it was he came from. And with a headache, a cracked shin, and painfully crushed nether-parts, it wasn't going to be pleasant.

I went back to the cabin. In the big, frugally furnished living-room I found Frederik fussing over Rebecca who had an ugly bruise across her cheek.

'They hit you,' I gasped.

'It's nothing,' she said.

'Who were they?' I asked.

Old Frederik turned to face me. 'We owe thee great gratitude. Thou saved us without a doubt.'

We stood there in the austere room, all in our night attire, Rebecca with a bruised face, old Frederik looking totally dishevelled – and me, in a dead man's nightshirt, with one hand in a bandage, the other gripping a six-shooter. And on the wall, an embroidered cloth proclaiming: BLESS THOSE WHO PERSECUTE THEE; BLESS AND DO NOT CURSE. But we were in no mood to bless anybody. 'Who were they?' I repeated.

'The Lawson brothers,' Rebecca explained. 'They were drunk and had heard stories of the bank robbery in town. They suspected Jason was here and that there would be a reward if they could catch him. They probably mistook thee for Jason. But I do not think they will come back, thanks to thee, Linus. I am sorry I made thee go through the window. I should have guessed there would be somebody waiting out there.' Then her eyes took on concern as she saw the blood on my nightshirt. 'Thou have been hit!'

I'd almost forgotten. I unfastened the top of my nightshirt, eased it back from my shoulder. 'Bullet just nicked me,' I said. 'Just grooved the flesh a bit.'

'I will make a poultice of milk and linseed oil,' she said. 'It will ease it,' and soon I was seated at the large plain-wood table while she fussed over me. Meanwhile, old Frederik bolted the door and secured the cabin, making sure all the shutters were across. There was always the chance those Lawson brothers might not be as scared as they pretended.

As Rebecca's gentle hands soothed the gash on my shoulder, I realized that I was enjoying her closeness, her efficient yet compassionate touch. I also noticed her bruising. 'How did your face get so battered?' I enquired.

She sighed. 'That Samuel Lawson does not know his own strength, particularly when the liquor has got into him. I told him to leave us alone, that Jason was not here. He took offence, called me a nasty name and hit me . . .'

'Just like Daddy used to . . .' It was young Ella piping up. She had been standing watching her mother at work.

'Shush!' Rebecca said. 'Thou should be in bed.'

Ella gave her mother a glare, then she said, 'Sorry, Mama,' and went to her room.

The Pinkerton Man

I probably had no right to probe, but the girl's words had surprised me. 'Your husband used to hit you?' I enquired.

Rebecca frowned, secured the bandage around my shoulder, then she nodded. 'Kaspar had a weakness for liquor. He ignored the rules of our faith, though I should not speak ill of the dead. Things were very difficult between us . . . yes, *very* difficult. But now he is gone and he cannot harm us any more.'

I didn't press her further. It was a private matter, none of my business, and yet I took some solace in the fact that her husband's death had not left her totally inconsolable.

But now it was old Frederik who joined the conversation. 'Kaspar was bad right from the time he was a babe. His mother had a difficult time birthing him, what with dropping two at the same time. Kaspar somehow got his head squeezed when he came into this world; I think it turned his brain. Now he is walking with God and we must pray that he will be forgiven for his sins and find peace.'

'I hope so,' I murmured. I wondered if God would also forgive me mine. I looked at Rebecca. 'You have been kind to me. Now you must let me bathe your face.'

She smiled. 'I would like that, Linus.'

Later, we went to our respective beds, but I kept the gun on my side table in case those Lawsons came back. I knew I'd been lucky with the bullet only grazing my shoulder, but it was sore despite the poultice and Rebecca's care. My thoughts returned to my injured hand: it had taken a pummelling this night and thoughts of the awful decision I would have to make troubled me. I wondered how long I would be obliged to keep up this pretence regarding my true identity. And what would I do if and when Jason returned? I had been fortunate tonight, getting the better of the intruders. Had they not been drunk it could have been a different matter. Once I came face to face with Jason, the moment of truth would have arrived, and disabled as I was, my chances of apprehending him would be decidedly slim. Furthermore, I would be betraying the hospitality and kindness of this family. And yet what option did I now have?

SIX

For the remainder of that night, I agonized over my circumstances. Despite my strenuous action at the time of the Lawsons' visit, I was still a sick man. My hand and arm were one centre of throbbing discomfort, not to mention the sore groove in my shoulder where the bullet had nicked me. I felt sure the latter would heal, but I feared that the hand injury wouldn't go away until the surgeon's knife went to work. Of course I still hoped and prayed that a miracle might descend on me, that Rebecca and Ella's prayers might bring a posse of healing angels down from Heaven, but I knew that was a long shot. Rebecca kept me dosed up with the old man's opium mixture, and I drifted in and out of a woozy state. I remembered the doctor's fluttering nostrils, and now I did my own share of sniffing, convinced that a putrid, gamy smell emanated from beneath the bandage of my hand. Tomorrow, I told myself, tomorrow I would ask Rebecca to take me to town and get the job done.

Next morning I got up from the bed and dressed, telling myself that, after the events of the previous night, I had no right to consider myself bed-ridden. Rebecca strove her best to take my mind off the suffering, trying to cheer me up with all her sweet nature. I hadn't had too much experience with women in my life, but I sensed that she was a special person and her presence and compassion were like a soothing balm to me, even her strange religious convictions.

Rebecca showed me her pigeon coop. She had about a dozen birds, white-plumed, plump and long-billed, and she spoke of them and fondled them as if they were children. 'Six of them belong to Seth Pilgrim, the postmaster in town,' she explained. 'When we want to send a message we free one and it flies home to him, and when I go to town I take some of my birds for when he has a message for us, like the news of the bank robbery. It is so much quicker than the ordinary mail, us being so remote out here.'

I nodded. She was a woman of many interests and skills, and this was illustrated a moment later when she showed me how she made butter.

She had a pail full of cream which she had left standing. She sniffed at it and said, 'It has to be sour but not rancid. This is just right.'

She poured it into a churn and we took turns at agitating it with an old hand-paddle, me working awkwardly with my left hand. Gradually, granules of butter formed, thickening up like scrambled egg, until there were enough to drain off the buttermilk. Rebecca worked the residue vigorously with the hand-paddle, forcing out the remaining moisture and forming convenient-sized blocks of butter.

The Pinkerton Man

'I take it to town to sell,' she explained, 'along with honey, eggs, vegetables and cantaloupes. When the wheat crop failed, that's all we had to get by on.'

She scooped a little butter on to her finger and held it out for me to lick which I did.

'What do thou think?' she enquired.

'It's sweet and it's beautiful, just like you, Rebecca.'

Her face flushed. 'Thou should not say such things. Me being freshly widowed and all.'

'I only speak the truth.'

Her embarrassment went as she smiled. 'I'd better change the dressing on thy hand.'

I nodded. The trusting look in her face made me squirm with guilt. I'd had no right to take advantage of these people, and yet I had plunged myself in so deep I shuddered at the outcome. I wished I could somehow hold back the passage of time, fend off the future.

I recalled my intention, during the night, to ask her to take me to the doctor's surgery in town. Now I decided to wait a little longer.

As we sat in the kitchen and she carefully removed my bandage and set to work, I asked a question I guess I had no right to. 'How come you married Kaspar van Bremer, Rebecca?'

She hesitated, then went back to work, answering in her candid way. 'I was sinful. I surrendered to temptation one evening after a picnic and . . . and I fell pregnant.' She busied herself with my bandage, keeping her head down.

'With Ella?' I asked.

'Yes, and Kaspar married me before my belly showed.'

'But things didn't work out between you?'

She sighed deeply, shook her head. 'He wasn't as I thought he was. He only paid lip service to the faith. He . . .' She looked up and her eyes were glistening with tears. 'I must not speak ill of the dead.'

'I'm sorry,' I said, 'I shouldn't have asked.'

'It is best thou know,' she said, though why this should be so I didn't enquire.

She fastened the bandage and looked up and she gave me such a warm smile, with her eyes still glistening, that my insides seemed to melt.

That afternoon, when I was sitting on the porch, Ella brought some books and asked me to read to her, which I did, hoping one day I would be a father myself with a sweet little girl like her. She perched on my knee and turned the pages, her wide-eyed attention riveted on my words despite my distinct impression that she knew the stories, word for word, already. 'Daniel in the Lions' Den', 'David and Goliath', 'Moses in the Basket'. And when I was finished she told me a story of her own, about a milk snake that that had been clinging to a cow's tit and Grandpa had been obliged to pull on its tail to make it let go. I asked her if she had actually seen it with her own eyes.

'Well, no,' she responded, 'but Grandpa told me.'

On the third day following the Lawsons' visit, I was in my usual place, sitting on the porch, back in the shadow and meditating on future action, when I heard one of the dogs give a joyous yelp, and glancing up I saw the dark figure of an approaching horseman – and instinct warned me that the moment of truth had arrived.

With the dogs running to greet the newcomer, old Frederik came out from the barn. ' 'Tis Jason,' he cried joyously. 'Thanks to the Lord that he is safe!'

I rose to my feet, glad that the old man had allowed me to carry a loaded gun in case the Lawsons reappeared. I'd slipped it into my waistband on the left side, even practised handling it when my hosts weren't looking. Now I feared that the weapon might be put to a use very different from that which old Frederik had imagined, although I was determined to avoid spilling blood if possible.

As Jason got near, he slipped from his claybank horse, the dogs leaping up. The sight of him sent a chill down my spine. The resemblance was uncanny. It was as if the man I had killed, Kaspar, had come back to haunt me. At first, he didn't see me. He only had eyes for his father and sister-in-law and little niece as they rushed out to embrace him. I was toying with the idea of immediately revealing myself as a Pinkerton, drawing my gun and attempting to arrest him. But seeing the joy of this family reunion, I hesitated – and suddenly old Frederik was saying, 'We have got a visitor, Jason. A friend of thine, I think. Linus Horne!'

For the first time, Jason became aware of my presence. His pale eyes lifted to mine and he said, 'Linus Horne.'

I just stood there, uncertainty clogging my every vein.

And then an astonishing thing happened. His bearded face widened into a smile, and he extended his hand and stepped up on to the porch. 'Sure is good to see thee! My, thou have taken a battering!'

His action had taken me completely by surprise. I opened my mouth to speak, but said nothing. I'd never seen this man before in my life, though he was the image of his late twin brother. He also resembled the old man. Now, his smile looked really genuine, and as I reached out with my left hand, he gave it a shake.

'Well, I never figured thou would make it here,' he went on. 'Figured thou had been killed along with Kaspar. Thou must take shelter here while thou get over that wound.'

'Jason,' old Frederik cut in. 'Did thou know about the bank raid in town.'

'No, Pa.'

'Well there are fellows who figure it was thy work. In fact the Lawsons came out here hunting for thee, saying they represented the law. But we sent them packing, thanks to Linus here. He scared the wits out of them.'

Jason gave me what appeared a grateful look and said, 'Well, I am truly beholden for that, Linus.'

I looked at his face, wondering about him. He was sure playing a strange game, and I knew I mustn't trust him for all his apparent candour.

I noticed how his face was all pimpled and he'd grown his beard extra thick in an unsuccessful attempt to conceal it. 'I used to have spots like that,' I said because I couldn't think of any more relevant words to come out with. 'But I got rid of them all by rubbing in Bale's Magic Liniment.'

'Bale's Magic Liniment,' he said thoughtfully, scratching his jaw. 'I must try that.'

Soon we were inside the cabin, and Rebecca was rustling up a meal. It was obvious that Jason had visited fairly recently, maybe only shortly before I arrived, and he must have imparted news of his brother's death, though he appeared not to know who had been behind the gun. At least that was the impression he was giving, but after we had bowed our heads and said our silent grace and were tucking into the food, I felt his pale eyes drifting over me. Maybe he was as desperate to fathom me out as I was him. I guess it was the weirdest meal I've ever experienced, despite the fact that Rebecca had worked wonders.

'How long are thou staying, son?', old Frederik enquired as he sliced bread into thick chunks.

'Well, if anybody gets an idea to come looking for me,' Jason replied, 'I guess I ought to be here so as not to disappoint them. I would not want anybody harming thee. Rebecca, that bruise on thy face. Who did that? I thought all that would be finished now.'

'Samuel Lawson,' she murmured. 'He was drunk, I guess.'

'If he meets up with me,' Jason said, 'he'll regret it.'

'No, Jason. Violence achieves nothing.'

I could not understand the drift of their conversation. How could the good-minded van Bremers provide sanctuary for this desperado – a man who had so far only escaped the law by blind luck?

The nagging thought was in me that I should push matters forward, that I should declare myself and take Jason in for the law to decide his fate. But still I hesitated. Call me a coward if you will.

During the following night the pain from my hand grew intense. I swore I could smell the gangrene. I figured unless I got matters sorted out, my condition would worsen and maybe kill me. I expressed my misery with a loud groan and Rebecca came and dosed me with the opium.

'Rebecca,' I gasped as I felt my senses drifting, 'will you take me to town tomorrow so that Dr O'Connell can do whatever is needed?'

'If that is what thou want then I will do it,' she murmured. 'And I will pray that the Lord will give thee strength, Linus.'

I hoped the Lord wouldn't get confused. It wasn't Linus who needed the strength; it was Frank – but I couldn't say so.

I felt pretty feverish next morning, with a burning, tingling feeling making my skin moist. Old Frederik roused me early. He always rose about 4.30 to milk the cows. Looking from the window at the pre-dawn, it seemed like a dream world out there, sinister and hostile. I wished I could hold back the passing hours. Feeling sick, I didn't fancy breakfast. Pork, eggs and freshly-baked bread, with a cup of creamy milk. I forced a little down, reckoning I was going to need all the strength I could get. Jason joined me at the breakfast table, wiping the sleep from his eyes and scratching his jaw. Soon he was tucking in, not sharing my lack of appetite.

'How come thou escaped when the others got killed?' he eventually enquired, and a quick panic rose in me.

'It was awful,' I said, striving to make my voice husky with anguish. 'Awful. Seeing them all shot down. Oh . . .' I subsided into grief, too emotional with the apparent memory of good friends being killed. Jason gave me a searching look, then appeared to get the message that I was in no condition to indulge in casual conversation.

He dragged his nails across his jaw. 'Maybe, whilst thou art in town, thou could order some of that Bale's Magic Liniment. These pimples are driving me crazy.'

After that he didn't say anything else.

Meanwhile Rebecca had prepared the family buggy and hitched a spirited black horse into its shafts. The buggy was nothing more than a black box on wheels, its narrow, bare-wood seat affording little comfort. Rebecca loaded her butter, jars of honey and eggs into the back. Twenty minutes later as we prepared to leave, old Frederik was surprisingly emotional. He put his arm around me and gave me a hug and wished the Lord's blessing on me. Jason afforded me a nod. I wondered what was backing his apparently easy-going nature.

Soon I was to find out.

SEVEN

Aboard that bone-jarring buggy, it was a three and a half hours' trip to town, moving between those awesome arches of rock. Each one was different, a miracle of elemental architecture. Sometimes we were completely in their shadow, after which we would come clear and burst into the sunshine again. Rebecca handled the reins with the expertise of a coach driver, the black horse stepping elegantly high. Rebecca's hair was plaited and coiled around beneath her dainty white bonnet and she wore the plainest of black dresses, black stockings, black shoes, all without the slightest of adornment. She didn't need adornment. Her simple yet radiant beauty was all she needed. In normal circumstances such a journey would have been a pleasure. The seat was so narrow that our bodies were wedged tightly together. But as the sun rose, the day became hot, and each bump in the trail sent shafts of pain shooting up my arm, and over me hovered the awful prospect of what Dr O'Connell had in store. Add to that, the brooding fear that the Lawson brothers might show up and make trouble for us, and you'll understand that I felt depressed and wretched.

'Maybe things will not be as bad as thou fear,' Rebecca murmured. 'We've prayed for thee really hard.' I sensed she was trying to convince herself just as much as she was me.

'The Lord moves in strange ways,' I said.

'He sees things that we are blind to.'

'You must scorn those who do not share your views,' I said. 'Those who are not of your faith.'

'We do not,' she responded firmly. 'Hanna people are no better than anybody else. But we are different . . . and we are separate.'

I nodded, touched by her conviction and having no wish or cause to doubt her sincerity.

I gripped my gun tightly with my left hand, scanning both sides of the trail as best I could through the square side-windows. Several times, my pulse quickened as riders appeared, but each time they proved to be nothing more than casual passers-by, some of them even touching their hats to Rebecca.

'When we get to town, Linus,' she advised, 'keep thy hat pulled low. We don't want the sheriff recognizing thee.'

It was mid-morning when we pulled into God's Navel and straight away we sensed that something was wrong because the place was deathly quiet, shimmering and silent in the torrid sun; all the stores were locked up, and no horses were tied to the hitch rails, no wagons or buckboards on the street, no townspeople making their way along the plank sidewalks. I wiped the sweat on my face, smearing it like a dust-cake.

Rebecca halted the wagon in front of the doctor's drugstore, touched my shoulder, then climbed down. She stepped up on to the porch and went in through the half-open door. A moment later she reappeared. 'Linus, come quick!'

I dropped from the wagon and followed her into the drugstore. We went through the waiting-room, where straight-backed chairs lined the walls. In the back room, the consulting room, we found Dr O'Connell slumped face down on the floor, alongside his couch, a big blowfly buzzing about his head.

'Is he dead?' Rebecca gasped.

I dropped to my knees, fanned the fly away and felt his pulse. 'Not dead,' I said, 'but he's got a mighty high temperature.'

Right then he emitted a groan.

'Let's put him on his back,' I said. 'See if we can find a cushion for his head.'

She nodded. Together we struggled to roll his cumbersome body over and I loosened his collar while Rebecca fetched a cushion to make him as comfortable as possible.

He opened his eyes, and they were bloodshot and running with moisture. He looked feverish and sallow. His voice came with a husky weakness. 'Damned influenza. The whole town's gripped by it. I thought I'd escaped, but this morning it started in me, headache, pains all over, and I guess I collapsed. I . . .' His voice trailed off.

Rebecca straightened up and went through an inner door. When she returned she said, 'There's a bed next door. Let's see if we can get him on to it.'

I nodded and we went to work. It wasn't easy, me only having one arm to work with, but Rebecca showed remarkable strength and somehow we shifted him through the doorway and got him into his bed.

'Does he have a wife or family?' I enquired.

She shook her head. 'Confirmed bachelor.'

After a while, he rallied slightly and mumbled, 'Yesterday I telegraphed to Salt Springs for medical support. Don't know when or if it will get here. Maybe they got the same trouble there.'

'You try to rest,' I told him. 'We'll keep an eye on things until help arrives.'

'No,' he gasped. 'You should get out, otherwise you'll get sick like the rest of us. By coughing or sneezing, even talking, one person can pass it to the next.'

'We'll not leave thee in this state,' Rebecca announced, settling the issue.

'We'll heat some water,' I said. 'A hot mustard foot-bath may help.'

O'Connell gave me a whimsical look. 'You should've been a doctor, Linus Horne. There's mustard in the kitchen cupboard.'

He started to cough and as I bathed his feet, Rebecca boiled a kettle and filled the room with steam which seemed to help him. Later, I pulled off his shirt and we sponged down his flabby body as best we could. I'd thought my fever was bad enough, but it was nothing compared with his. I'd never seen a man so on fire as he was. As per his instructions, we dosed him with some spirits of camphor.

It was crazy, maybe wicked, but I have to admit I felt somewhat relieved right then. In his sick state Dr O'Connell was in no fit condition to carry out major surgery. Maybe fate had decreed that I could keep my hand.

Over the next hours I had little alternative but to put my own problems in abeyance. The seriousness of the situation was rammed home to me when I stepped outside the back door of the place, glanced down a side alley and saw four coffins lined up against a wall. The whole town seemed bathed in an eerie silence. I unhitched the black horse from the buggy and took him across to the town's livery. There was nobody there apart from a few more horses, but I found my animal a stall and rubbed him down, then I fetched some feed for him.

Afterwards, I took a brief stroll around the deserted town. Everywhere was shut, the school house, the stores. The bank apppeared closed for different reasons from everywhere else. A poster on the window proclaimed: BANK CLOSED BECAUSE OF ROBBERY. Only one place showed any sign of life, and that was the sheriff's office and jail; I saw the sheriff standing on the boardwalk outside, vigorously drawing on a large cigar. Under the circumstances I thought it was best I should avoid him, so I dodged back the way I'd come. Presently, I saw a couple of women who were hurrying along with handkerchiefs over their faces, and as they went by I smelt the sharp tang of disinfectant. The post office, like everywhere else, was closed, but I heard the coo of pigeons from the back and wondered if birds could withstand the influenza.

Rebecca and I stayed overnight with the doctor, caring for him as best we could. I insisted that Rebecca rested on the medical couch. I sat out the hours on the hard seats of his waiting-room, managing to snatch some sleep. Come morning, I awoke feeling stiff and in pain, but I forced myself up and stretched and Rebecca joined me, looking unbelievably cool and unflustered.

The doctor was showing a slight improvement and his temperature had dropped. He even took a little sustenance.

On his shelf was a range of medicines and I spotted a small bottle of Bale's Magic Liniment. I thought of Jason and his spots. I asked O'Connell if I might buy it, but he said to take it for free. It was the least he could do after all we'd done for him.

Later on, he told us how the influenza epidemic had struck the town ten days ago. The first mortality was an elderly woman, and he had thought it was pneumonia, but four more people were later stricken and passed away, and as more cases developed he diagnosed the influenza epidemic. He had done his best, isolating patients as much as possible, giving them mustard baths and dosing them with spirits of camphor. But three more deaths had followed, including two children, and the whole town had adopted a siege mentality.

But today, mid-morning brought relief. A stagecoach pulled into town, the thud of hooves and the creak and rattle of the wheels cutting through the quietness as if intent on rousing the dead. The coach halted outside. A tall man with a leather bag climbed stiffly down, followed by three matronly ladies. Obviously the awaited medical assistance had arrived. Soon O'Connell was relating in a gasping voice his tale of woe to the newcomer, Dr Henry Warwick, and the latter rapidly issued instructions to his ladies. They were weary after their overnight journey from Salt Springs, but without complaint they went out into the town, setting about bringing relief to stricken homes, regardless of the risk of infection to themselves. Dr Warwick even found time to glance at me and comment, 'What happened to you?' His eyes were resting on my bandaged arm.

'Just a scratch,' I responded, being too cowardly to face up to a further medical examination right now. As a matter of fact, I'd temporarily almost forgotten my own pain.

Warwick gave me a 'try pulling the other one' look, but he was too busy to press the matter further.

Rebecca fetched the provisions she'd intended to sell, and gave them to Warwick, asking him to distribute them amongst the needy.

I turned to her and said, 'Best thing we can do is get back to the cabin.'

She hesitated, no doubt wondering if she could be of assistance here, but then said, 'Maybe thou art right.'

So we bade our farewells to the two doctors, wished them well. A moment later I was helping Rebecca hitch up the black horse to the buggy, outside the livery. We both felt pretty tired after our less than restful time, and I prayed to God that we hadn't picked up the influenza. I wondered how long it took to reveal itself. We were almost ready to pull out when I heard Rebecca's sharp intake of breath, and turning I saw a man with a gun covering me. A big cigar protruded from his mouth, the cloud of its smoke about him, and there was a silver star pinned to his shirt. Town Sheriff Sam Crofton.

'Raise your hands, Linus Horne,' he snapped out. 'You won't be leaving town today!' His eyes were dark and set deep under thick black brows.

I felt stunned. This was the last thing I'd expected. All I could do was raise my good hand in submission as Rebecca looked on in dismay.

'He's been badly hurt,' she said. 'He's in no condition to be arrested. He's done no harm, only good.'

Crofton laughed scornfully. 'Try telling that to a judge. Next to the Childeater, Linus Horne was the worst killer in the gang.' His eyes flicked over my bandaged arm. 'Maybe I can't handcuff you, but I won't have no hesitation in shooting you down if you try any tricks. Now get walking across to the jail.' He jerked his gun aggressively.

I exchanged an alarmed glance with Rebecca. She'd gone pale, her lips a tight line of concern.

'You'd better go home,' I said to her. 'There's nothing you can do here now.'

'I'll not leave thee,' she argued.

'Rebecca,' I said firmly, 'Ella and Frederik need you at home.' I didn't mention Jason in fear that the sheriff would have him arrested.

Still Rebecca hesitated.

'Please go home,' I insisted. 'I'll sort things out here.'

'Like hell you will,' Sheriff Crofton cut in harshly.

'Please Rebecca,' I repeated.

She gave me a helpless look and quietly said, 'As thou wish,' and then she added, 'Do get that new doctor to examine thine arm,' and then she dropped her voice and added, 'God bless thee, Linus.'

While she climbed aboard the buggy, the sheriff relieved me of my gun. Rebecca flicked the reins and the horse trotted forward. She didn't look back. For a second we watched her moving down the deserted street, swirling up the dust as she gathered speed, then Crofton nudged me with his gun. 'Start walking,' he ordered. 'You don't deserve the friendship of such a sweet woman.'

And at that moment I guessed he was right.

EIGHT

As we trudged down the street, passing closed-up stores, his gun prodding my back, I asked, 'How come you knew I was Linus Horne?'

He grunted impatiently. 'I'll ask the questions around here, not you.'

I ignored his surliness. 'And how come you haven't caught the influenza, same as everybody else in town?'

This time he deigned to give me an answer. 'The way to stay healthy in an epidemic, is to smoke cigars. Rich Havanas. Surround yourself with cigar smoke and it scares the bugs away.'

'Maybe you could spare one of those cigars for me then,' I said.

'You don't deserve no consideration, mister!'

Five minutes later I was locked in one of the tiny cells behind his office. The heat was stifling and now I felt that with every breath, I was contaminating myself with influenza.

Sheriff Crofton was in no mood for conversation. Through the cell bars I could see him scribbling away at his desk, no doubt writing out a report as to how he'd apprehended the notorious Linus Horne. I debated on the wisdom of revealing my true identity. I concluded that I possessed no proof of my actual self and no string of words would convince him that I was a Pinkerton man. The only way he could confirm my identity was to telegraph the Pinkerton headquarters, and with the post office closed down there was no way he could do that. So I decided to play along with him for a while. Maybe I might learn a thing or two if I didn't die of influenza. I wondered how he felt so sure I was Linus Horne. The real Linus was dead and buried up in north Utah, but somebody must have informed him that I was the outlaw. And, so far as I knew, and discounting little Ella, there were just four people who believed, or pretended to believe, that I was Linus: old Frederik, Rebecca, Dr O'Connell . . . and Jason van Bremer. I couldn't bring myself to suspect that old Frederik or Rebecca had betrayed me. Dr O'Connell had been in no condition to inform the sheriff I was in town. That left only Jason, and being on the run himself, he'd hardly have been in communication with a lawofficer. The situation didn't make sense.

I soon got tired of sitting in that airless, dreary jail. Crofton was utterly uncommunicative, spending most of his time, so far as I could discern, standing out on his veranda, puffing on his cigar. But later on, when he brought me a plate of stringy beef and stale bread and filled my water jug, taking no chances as he passed it through the bars, he struck me as being decidedly shaky on his feet and there was a tremble in his hands. It worried me. Maybe he was sickening with the influenza. Maybe his cigar smoke was as useless in warding off the bugs as I thought it was. If he collapsed, I would be trapped in this cage. So I decided I would gain nothing by staying here. It was time to move matters forward.

'Sheriff,' I said as he was turning back towards his office, 'I guess you've made a mistake.'

'Uh?' He gave me a blank look.

'I'm not Linus Horne. I'm a Pinkerton detective posing as an outlaw.'

I didn't think he had it in him to laugh, but he did – a long, scornful bray. 'Tell that to the judge!'

'What made you think I was Linus Horne?' I asked.

'I have an informant, mister, but I ain't telling you who, so don't try your tricks.'

'Well the informant was wrong, and I can prove it.'

'You just do that,' he said mockingly.

'You telegraph the Pinkerton headquarters. Tell them I claim to be Frank S. Glengarry. I'll give you my license number.'

'Won't be no telegrams going out from here,' he said. 'Not with the post office closed down.'

'Well, as soon as it opens up, will you send one?'

He hesitated. I could see he was running a fever despite his bravado.

'Will you?' I repeated.

He was shaking his head from side to side in disbelief, but he shuffled off, saying, 'Maybe ... maybe not.'

I suffered the rest of the day feeling totally frustrated. He seemed to spend most of his time slumped over his desk in the main office, and I could just see him down the corridor. In the evening he disappeared for a while and when he came back he said his wife had gone down with influenza and the doctor and nurses were attending to her. I gathered that he had a house on the outskirts of town. Another fellow with a gun joined him. He was scrawny and as skinny as a broomstick. He brought me some supper, and he kept me covered with his gun, while the sheriff emptied my slop pale. The newcomer, despite his matchstick physique, looked as if he knew how to handle that gun, so I didn't feel an attempt at escape was on the cards. I resigned myself to spending the night behind bars. I hoped that the sheriff would remain on his feet until the post office reopened and that telegram could be sent.

Everything went quiet, until presently I heard some coyotes yip-yapping from the outskirts. The town seemed like a morgue, which maybe it was in many respects. I wondered how that new doctor and his team were coping and if they were avoiding contamination themselves – not by smoking cigars, that was for certain.

After a dreary night, the sheriff brought me some breakfast and later he told me that the post office had reopened and, just to call my bluff, he'd send off that telegram. With shaky fingers he jotted down my license number and the other details I gave him, then he left me. He was walking like a drunk, but I was sure it wasn't the liquor affecting him.

I never saw him again.

I spent the rest of that seemingly endless morning in that cell, listening to the buzz of flies and aware once more of the throbbing pain in my hand. The dressing should have been changed long since. I guessed the sheriff had been taken ill, so ill he'd probably forgotten my existence. I strained against the bars but found them totally unyielding. From outside, I heard the occasional movement of wagons in the street, but nobody came near the jail. For all the good it was to me, the rest of the town, what was left of it, might just as well have been on another planet. I was getting mighty desperate – and then at last I had a visitor. It was the skinny fellow who had helped the sheriff last evening. I noticed he was carrying the keys to my cell. He told me what I had suspected.

'Fred Crofton has gone down with the influenza, same as his wife.'

'Must've been using the wrong brand of cigars,' I commented.

'I guess you'll be interested in this,' he said. He passed a paper through the bars for me to read. It was a telegram. The sheriff had obviously despatched what I had suggested to Pinkerton headquarters and this was the reply.

YOU ARE HOLDING FRANK S. GLENGARRY PINKERTON
UNDERCOVER OPERATIVE. RELEASE IMMEDIATELY.
SIGNED ROBERT PINKERTON.

Within five minutes I was out of that darned jail, collecting my gunbelt from the sheriff's desk on the way. I had just one immediate intention: to get away from this sick place. I went to the town livery, which I found deserted apart from the horses in the stalls. I selected a sturdy-looking roan and found a saddle and bridle. I also found some paper and a pencil and in my spidery left-handed scrawl, I explained that I had taken the animal and tackle and would they kindly bill the Pinkerton Detective Agency. I had no intention of being strung up for horse theft. Soon I was riding up the deserted street. I didn't see a soul, though there was movement behind the odd window.

I was well beyond the outskirts when I reined in and gave consideration to my best course of action. Jason van Bremer was an enigma to me. Why hadn't he blown my pretence sky high? Surely he must've known I was not the real Linus Horne. What were his motives? The whole thing had me perplexed. But I realized my instructions to arrest him still stood firm, and maybe it was my duty to do just that. So I heeled my animal forward, taking the trail towards the van Bremers' remote smallholding. I had to admit that something else was drawing me back as well: thoughts of Rebecca. In fact it was more than 'thoughts'. It was a desperation. Something I'd never felt for a woman before.

I don't know why, but as I got nearer to the homestead, I felt overwhelmed with a feeling of doom, a breathless urge to push the roan hard, to keep my stops to a minimum. Maybe I'd been conditioned to expect the worst over the past days, but that didn't make it rest any easier in my mind. Evening was taking hold, lengthening the shadows of the looming rocks, as I rode onward. The feeling was in me that time was of the essence, that I had to get back to Rebecca as quickly as I could.

Two hours after leaving God's Navel, night had closed in, and it was then that I smelt an acridity in the air and my throat constricted with fear. I could taste ash as I drew in breath. As I topped the last rise and went down through the trees, close to where I'd first spied on the homestead, I saw a glimmer of flame ahead, not the high leap of flame – but the redder low smoulder of a conflagration that had already done its wicked work, and the air was thickened with smoke. There was a staleness about it and I sensed that it had spread and hung on the air for some hours.

I gasped with anguish, goaded the lathered roan down the slope with one final spurt. There was sufficient moonlight to see that the stone walls of the cabin still stood erect, but from within these the redness of smouldering timber glowed, all that remained of the place's furnishings and wooden fixings. The cabin was a shell; the entire interior and all it had contained were gutted. The stone chimneystack, blackened and gaunt, reared against the sky like a sombre tombstone.

I guessed there were tears in my eyes, partly from the sting of the smoke, but more so from the despair that weighed upon me like a sack of rocks. I slid from the saddle and forced my way through increasing heat. Stumbling over something, I looked down and saw it was the lifeless body of the white dog,

Snowy, my one-time companion. Even in the dim light I could see that he was riddled with bullets. A moment later I stood, choking on the ash, feeling the heat scorching up through the soles of my boots; close enough to know that there could be no living soul left within this ruin. For a long moment, I closed my eyes, and gave way to deep, shuddering wretchedness. Rebecca, the old man, little Ella . . . were they all dead? Were their remains cremated to ash and mingled with the smouldering timber before me? I felt sickened. Rebecca . . . my God, I had loved her, right from the first time I'd set eyes upon her. Now. . . ?

I strove to get my emotions under control. I got my eyes open, wiped them with my sleeve. I swung my gaze around. All the outbuildings had been reduced to charred ruins, even the pigeon coop. And then something drew my attention . . . something that lay like a discarded cloth doll just within the fringe of shadow and I stumbled across and discovered the body. Old Frederik, in his nightshirt, was sprawled on his back, his sightless eyes gazing towards the moon. I leaned over him and saw the bullet hole in his forehead. The breath escaped me in a tremulous sigh. Frederik . . . once, I had imagined him an enemy, but he had subsequently proved to be a good friend. His motive had been nothing more than a Christian desire to help somebody in dire circumstances, no matter whether they were good or bad. God rest his soul!

Rebecca . . . what had happened to her? I moved through the shadows, terrified that I would find more bodies. But I circled the cabin, straining my eyes in the gloom, and the only corpses I encountered were those of beasts: a cow and hogs, and the two dogs, all riddled with bullets. The fencing of the corral had been smashed down, most of the horses were long gone, but the motionless hulks of two animals remained. I went closer. One of the dead horses was my faithful dun, Jack. He had been shot in the head. I cursed the devil who had done this.

A dreadful conclusion descended over me. Rebecca and Ella had either been burned to death, or carried off by the fiends who had brought havoc to this peaceful homestead. Maybe the first possibility was the more merciful of the two.

I would have slumped to the ground then, overwhelmed by helplessness and grief, but I didn't get the chance because I heard the metallic click of a gun's hammer being thumbed back and the voice cut through the darkness behind me, causing me to jerk with shock. It came angry, trembling, tinged with hysteria. 'Don't move, Linus Horne. One false move and I will shoot thee dead, so help me God!'

NINE

I froze. I didn't turn. I had no doubt that the man holding the gun meant what he said. I also had no doubt that he was Jason van Bremer.

'Thou might have escaped jail, but thou will not escape me.' He was struggling to bridle his fury, his natural lust to avenge what he misguidedly believed had happened. 'Thou have killed my father. Why haven't thou run off with thy murdering friends?'

'What friends?' I asked.

'Thou know full well I mean the Childeater, may his soul burn in hell! And thine too!'

'You mean the Childeater set fire to this place, killed your father?'

He didn't answer. He didn't need to.

'But why should the Childeater have done this?' I asked.

'Thou know full well.'

'No,' I groaned. 'I had no knowledge of this. You see . . . I'm not Linus Horne.'

I heard him grunt with disbelief. After a second he said, 'Thy lies will achieve nothing.'

'I swear I'm Frank Glengarry. I'm a Pinkerton agent. I pretended I was Horne.'

There was a pause while he digested my revelation. I could hear him grinding his teeth. I didn't know whether he was going to believe me or not.

I pressed on. 'You say the Childeater did this. Why?'

He ignored my question. 'Thou art trying to trick me. Thou art Linus Horne. Turn around slowly.'

I complied, seeing his dark shadow standing up-slope from me, sensing the emotion, the anger, that emanated from it.

'Why should the Childeater have burned this place?' I repeated.

He hesitated, debating whether he should trust me or not. 'Thou know full well, he was trying to get revenge on me,' he said, 'but I wasn't here, so he did what he thought would hurt me the most. He torched our home, killed my father.'

His words didn't make much sense, but there was something else I had to know. 'Rebecca and the little girl? Are they dead?'

He emitted a deep sigh. 'They might just as well be. He's kidnapped them both. God only knows what he'll do to them.'

I cursed.

'Why did thou come here?' he asked.

'I had orders to arrest you on charges of robbery and murder.'

For a long moment he just stared at me, then suddenly he appeared to relent. 'A Pinkerton man. Who would have thought.' He sighed deeply, then went on. 'I wasn't guilty, mister. Never was. Maybe if I'll believe thy story, thou will believe mine. Then we can get my father buried.'

'It's a deal,' I murmured. 'I've only got one good hand, but I'll do my best.' And to my relief he was slipping his gun back into its holster.

With difficulty but with reverence, we carried the old man's body away from the cabin and down to the meadow where there was already a cross erected over a grave. 'My mother's,' he grunted huskily. 'We'll bury him next to her.'

We had no spades, but we found some wood and scraped at the soil, and it seemed to take us hours for the ground was hard, and all the while my thoughts were on Rebecca and Ella, now in the hands of the man known as Childeater, and every minute they were probably getting further and further away. But Jason remained intent on the task in hand and we toiled away until the hole was deep enough to accept his father. When we had filled the grave in, he knelt for a long time in silent prayer, his eyes clamped shut, his hands steepled before him, and it would have been the easiest thing in the world to club him down with the chunk of wood I had used to dig, but of course I could do no such thing. Maybe I should never have been a detective.

He finished and stood up, wiping his eyes. 'He was a good man. He deserved better sons than me and Kaspar. As soon as I can, I will have a proper coffin made for him and there'll be a proper funeral service.'

'Sure,' I said, 'but first let's help the living. Let's go find Rebecca and the little girl.'

He nodded. 'Come dawn we will pick up the trail, and pray to God we are not too late already.'

He was right. Without daylight we'd never find the tracks of those who had committed this horrific atrocity. If we started off now, we might head in the wrong direction. I wondered how many there were and how we could possibly outwit them.

Jason and I waited for the night hours to pass. He fetched his claybank horse and brought it to where I had tethered the roan.

'If we are to stand any chance of getting Rebecca and Ella back,' he said, 'we've got to trust each other.'

'Tell me one thing,' I said. 'Why did the Childeater burn your place? I thought you were part of his gang.'

'No,' he grunted, 'never was. Me and Kaspar always got mistook for each other, looking so alike. We each got blamed for what the other did. Everybody took it for granted that we operated together, got up to the same tricks, but it was not so. I am not an angel, Mr Glengarry, but I have never broken the law, not intentionally. But once Kaspar started going with the Childeater gang, he fell under the Childeater's influence and we all saw how that would end. I formed a pact with the sheriff. I tried to persuade Kaspar to come home, to quit the gang and maybe we could arrange some sort of pardon if he showed good will. But he would not hear of it.'

'Were you at the gunfight when the law jumped the gang up in the Uinta Mountains?'

'No,' he said. 'I had realized that nothing would

change his mind. I was staying in town when they brought the bodies in over the backs of horses. I saw Kaspar's body from my hotel window.'

'You didn't see me?' I asked.

He shook his head.

'I was part of the posse that jumped the gang,' I said.

He nodded again but said nothing. I did not enlarge on the matter. It was downright ironic: if what he said was true, and I had no reason to doubt him, the law had been wrong in suspecting him of the same crimes as his brother. In fact, we no longer had the original cause to be enemies, though if he knew the whole truth he might well have reason to hate my guts. One day, perhaps, I'd admit to him that it had been my bullet that killed his brother — but not yet.

I reached out my good hand, we shook, and I said, 'Like you said, Jason, we've got to trust each other.'

Looking back it seems crazy, but that's the way it was.

Soon, he was filling me in on his version of events. He had been returning home when he had seen flames licking the night sky. Riding closer, he discovered the cabin ablaze and spotted riders pulling away. He'd got near enough to recognize the Childeater, but had not been able to determine who the other riders were. There'd been about six of them, that was all, heading northward into the remoteness of the Arches. His thoughts had immediately turned to his father, Rebecca and Ella, and he'd rushed down to the blazing cabin. Maybe he'd risked his own life, battled his way into the scorching heat. Somehow he'd ascertained that nobody had perished amid the flames. It was after this that he found his father's body, and in a blaze of fury he'd given chase to the marauders – but in the darkness he'd been unable to pick up the tracks. Overcome with grief, he'd dismounted and rested up, anxious for the night hours to pass. Much later he'd decided to return to the homestead and bury his father. Before he could do this, he'd encountered me.

Now I let his words sink into my brain, and tried to fathom what made him tick.

'So it was you who informed the sheriff I was coming to town?' I said.

He nodded. 'I thought thou were Linus Horne. Sent a pigeon.'

I mulled over that for a while. In a way it proved he was telling the truth, adding to the reason he had given me for the Childeater burning the cabin, murdering old Frederik and absconding with Rebecca and her daughter.

Dawn came – a crimson sunrise streaked with gold flares, and for a moment the only sounds were the ratchet-like cries of squirrels. It was as if they were chattering about the hideous events of the previous day. When the light was sufficient, we picked up the tracks. The trail led us across hills, in and out of washes and along the spines of ridges. I was bleary-eyed and weary, my bandaged hand was just a numb block of misery, pain nagged up my right arm and seeped into my entire body; my dressing had needed changing long ago, the spot where the bullet had snagged me was sore, and I was covered in sweat and grime. Yet everything paled to insignificance compared with the pounding desire which was driving me on. The most important thing in the whole world was to rescue Rebecca and little Ella before they were brutalized by the fiend who held them captive. I was now certain of my own feelings. If Rebecca survived this ordeal, I would tell her everything, the whole truth about what had happened in the Uinta Mountains, and pray to God that she would not condemn me. And, if there was forgiveness in her heart, I would ask her to be my wife.

The day was overcast and there was an oppressive stillness in the air. But the trail was relatively easy to follow, the tracks marking the shale distinctly – at least for the first hours. The outlaw party had moved fast, showing evidence of only brief stops, and I wondered how Rebecca and Ella were coping with the pace, and where they were being taken. At one point where they had stopped, I found a piece of blue ribbon fastened to a thorn, and Jason said it had belonged to Ella. We suspected that Rebecca had left it in the hope that it might be found by anybody following. We felt encouraged and pressed on, but gradually the ground became more rocky and the tracks were less easily discerned. An armada of clouds had swung in low, multiplying and merging, piling up like sea foam to blot out the light. Lightning pierced the gloom, thunder cracked and presently the heavens opened to unleash a drenching rain which splattered into us like pellets and drew a beaded curtain across our front.

We were obliged to pull up and seek shelter beneath a rocky overhang. As we hunkered down, dripping and miserable, I could see that the loss of his father was gnawing at Jason. I thought of my own dad and knew how cut up I'd be when he went. I hoped he'd die peacefully in a bed and not be cut down by a maniac's bullet as poor Frederik had been.

Presently I noticed that Jason's lips were moving and I realized he was praying.

I glanced away, saw how the low grey ceiling of cloud hung over the rugged hills and valleys. Right now it looked totally forlorn and different from any other terrain I'd previously encountered, and I wondered if its vastness would swallow up those whom we followed, like grains of sand, and conceal them for evermore. The rain would have washed out most of the tracks, and the Childeater could have headed in any direction. One guess was as good as another. But Jason said there was a small town called Woodenshoe Gulch about twenty miles further north. He knew it because there was a Hanna community there. It was just possible that the outlaws were heading that way. We decided we didn't have much choice so, despite the rain, we pressed on, hunched in our ponchos, wet and dejected. For my own part, I was overwhelmed with a sense of helplessness. Our enemies could be miles away, possibly heading in a completely different direction. Alternatively, they might be watching the trail, sheltering behind rocks, their guns poised to cut us down. As for Jason, I couldn't tell what he was thinking. He'd lapsed into silence, but I saw a light burning in his eyes and it wasn't pleasant. For a Christian man, he sure had the ability to hate – and if fortune smiled on us and we did take our quarry unawares, the Childeater would have a fight on his hands, that was certain.

But the odds weren't encouraging.

TEN

Several times the sheer volume of rain forced us to seek shelter as we went on, following the scarcely discernible road. Water sluiced from the heavens, turning every gully into a raging torrent. My feelings had plummeted lower than ever and the future seemed as grim as the weather. But there was one burden that I felt I must shrug off. A feeling was growing in me that I must be absolutely straight with Jason concerning the death of his brother. I must find the courage to tell him the truth. I didn't know what his reaction would be. He might turn violent, might draw his gun; alternatively he might turn his back on me in disgust and ride away. As we crouched beneath a dreary overhang of grey slab rock, the rain thudding against its exposed top, the words rose to my lips like a bilious eruption.

'Jason, I need to tell you how Kaspar died.'

He sighed impatiently. 'I know how he died. Shot down by those lawmen at the cave hideout.'

'It was me who did the shooting.'

He gave me a shocked glance, opened his mouth to speak but no words came out.

'I killed your brother,' I repeated. 'He was taking aim at Sheriff Ollerton. I fired off my hand-gun. It was a lucky shot. He died instantly.'

'Oh Lord,' he said. He straightened up, went to his horse, mounted up. His hat was pulled low. I couldn't see his face. He touched his heels to the animal's flanks and rode forward, not looking back, not heeding the rain.

I too mounted up, followed along behind him. We didn't speak for the rest of the morning. The road led us through a complex of sand dunes, monoliths and hogback ridges. In between them, the ground was smitten by quicksands. At last the deluge relented, the sun poked through the clouds and presently the gnats came in swarms so that we were obliged to lift our bandannas over our faces.

By the time we reached Woodenshoe Gulch it was early afternoon. It lay on the south bank of a river, a street lined with white timber houses and stores. Old time buggies moved up and down the main street, and at the far end stood a church, a low, insignificant building with a simple cross upon its tin roof.

'Many Hanna folk live here,' Jason told me, at last breaking his silence. 'They will tell us if strangers are here or have passed through.'

I nodded, inwardly feeling relief. Maybe there was no forgiveness in his heart for what I'd done, but, in talking to me again, he seemed to have accepted the bitter truth.

As we rode up the street, I noticed how many of the people were garbed in the same old-world style that the van Bremers adopted. Jason knew some of them and exchanged greetings. There was a saloon, though it was extremely prim and not of the depraved type I was used to. While I was slaking my thirst on a welcome beer, drying myself out alongside a stove, and listening to a Scott Joplin tune being tinkled on the piano, Jason asked around about any strangers that had come through the town. He came back to me with a long face. 'No strangers have shown up here for over a month,' he said.

'They could have come this way but bypassed this town,' I said.

He shook his head dejectedly. 'Or we could be headed in the wrong direction. I reckon we best stay here for tonight. There is a guest-house down the street.'

I nodded. The situation was getting more bleak by the minute.

When we were ensconced in the guest-house, I took a welcome bath, and eased the soiled bandage away from my hand. The sight which met my eyes depressed me still further. I knew that, no matter what happened, I would never have the use of my right hand again. It was disfigured, with the thumb lying like a shrivelled twig in my palm. The flesh had a sickly green shade and it was seeping and rotting. I washed it as best I could and Jason acquired some clean bandage and helped me wrap it round, and I wondered how much it hurt to have your hand cut off. Then I started to wonder about Rebecca and Ella. I felt certain they would not have the pleasure of soaking in a bath. I wondered if Rebecca had been raped and abused and the thought made me groan with anguish.

The guest house was spartan but clean, with religious tracts decorating otherwise bare walls. The place was typical of the Hanna way of life. We were weary, but even so I couldn't sleep. Next morning when we were finishing breakfast, we heard the chime of a church bell and Jason realized it was the Sabbath. 'I'll go to church,' he said. 'I've got some prayers that need saying.'

I nodded. 'I've got a few things I want to sort out with the Lord myself. Are visitors welcome?'

He gave me a strange look. 'Sure they are, Frank.'

Soon we were out in the street, joining the flock of Hanna folk, all in their Sunday best, going to the church. I felt downright out of place in my travel-soiled clothing, but nobody else seemed to worry.

I had never attended a church service like this one. Women and men were separated by the middle aisle. No children were present. For the first half-hour everybody stood in total silence, presumably for inner prayer and meditation, after which several of the congregation came forward and confessed to sins and asked forgiveness. The minister, in his dark suit and rough collar, gave them penances and his blessing, and told them to sin no more. He then preached in a strange-sounding language. Later I learned it was Pennsylvania Dutch – a sort of mixture of Palatine German and English. Despite only understanding about a third of his words, I got the impression he was administering a grim warning about sins of the flesh. And then the congregation joined in a repetitive chant, again in the Pennsylvania Dutch language. Finally, most of the worshippers removed their shoes, including Jason, and went forward to dip their feet in a low trough of water, men first, women following. All the time, I had the feeling that the minister was hurrying things along, and when the service was finished, he was the first out of the church. By the time we followed suit, he was racing out of town in a buggy.

'Minister is on wedding duty up at Salvation Bluffs,' somebody commented.

We nodded and decided to return to the guest-house and review our plans with the aid of our map. My feeling of gloom had not lifted. It seemed we had been grasping at straws and achieved nothing. There was no telling where the Childeater had gone, where he had taken Rebecca and Ella – or even if they were still alive. Back at the guest-house, we spread the map on the table and tried to put ourselves in the boots of the outlaws. They might well have headed deep into the remotest areas of Arches country, perhaps hidden up in some secret cave. With the trail gone cold, finding them would be akin to tracing the proverbial needle in a haystack. But I had overlooked one thing.

The fact that the Good Lord had listened to our prayers.

We studied our map for the best part of an hour and were torn between the ideas of heading west or east. Eventually, we decided to take a chance and head deeper into the Arches, hoping we might stumble across some evidence of our quarry.

With this decided, Jason said he wished to visit a friend who lived on the far side of the community. While he was gone I sat back in a rocking-chair, still weary from my vexed night's sleep. Soon I had dozed off. Nobody disturbed me. When I awoke, I checked my pocket watch. I'd slept without dreams for over three hours.

I was climbing to my feet, stretching, when Jason came rushing in, his face flushed with excitement. 'I just got some news, Frank. My friend told me the minister had gone to Salvation Bluffs to officiate in a couple of weddings. One was between a Hanna girl and a person who was not of our faith.'

'Well?'

'The man's name was Nathaniel Kirby.'

'Kirby!' I gasped. 'That's the Childeater's real name.'

'We must move quickly,' Jason said.

I rammed on my hat. Within minutes we had gathered up our belongings and had rushed to the hostlery to saddle our animals. This was the first real clue we'd had for days, and the implications were alarming. Was Rebecca about to marry the Childeater? Why on earth had she consented, or was she being forced into it?

In normal circumstances, it would have taken us three hours to ride to Salvation Bluffs, but having encouraged us, Fate dealt us a cruel blow. We'd gone no more than ten miles when Jason's claybank trod in a pothole and went down, catapulting Jason over his neck. I was riding ahead at the time, but hearing the commotion I reined in and turned my roan. Both man and horse were lying on their backs. Sliding from my saddle, I approached Jason and crouched down at his side. I reckoned he had struck his head in the fall and the awful impression was in me that he was dead, but suddenly he groaned and his eyes flicked open. I fetched my canteen, uncorked it and touched it to his lips. He took a little water, tried to speak, but was too dazed. Then we both heard the anguished snort of the fallen horse. I rose and went to the beast. The sight of its foreleg, the whiteness of shattered bone poking through the flesh, was distressing. Meanwhile, Jason had somehow climbed to his feet, had tottered across to join me. He crouched down, ran a comforting hand across the animal's head, then he straightened up and gave me a grim nod. 'It has to be done, Frank,' he said.

I nodded and drew my gun. It was a task I hated, but we had no option. I can only pride myself with the fact that it was an instant kill, that the beast suffered no more. We would have to leave the carcass for the buzzards.

Jason himself was immensely shaken. He'd taken a bad bruising in the fall, but appeared not to have broken any bones. He stripped his saddle from the dead animal, hoisted it across his shoulder, then we both climbed on to the back of my already weary roan and pressed on. The going was slow, the ground still wet and slippery, the air filled with the contrapuntal croaking of windbag frogs celebrating the moistness. We had to stop on numerous occasions to rest the horse. I grew conscious of the time slipping away, of the sun drifting into the west and the fear grew in me that we would be too late. Even if we arrived at Salvation Bluffs in time, what could we do? The prospect of gunning a man down as he stood at the altar on his wedding day, standing before God in holy matrimony, was abhorrent, yet what alternatives were there? Of course there was also the possibility that Rebecca had chosen of her own free will to marry the outlaw, though it seemed inconceivable, yet I knew the workings of the human mind were often incomprehensible. The thought made me shudder.

We topped the hill overlooking Salvation Bluffs in the late afternoon. Jason had not visited the place previously, though he knew it was one of the three main Hanna communities in the territory.

The church, another low structure with a cross, was midway up the main street, and there were several horses and buggies hitched to the rail outside. My heart was hammering as we slid from the back of the weary roan and mounted on to the porch of the church. From inside I could hear scuffling sounds. It was obvious that a service was in progress. I loosened my gun in its holster as we passed through the open doorway and stepped into the shadowed interior. The church was crowded, men and women on separate sides of the aisle, but nobody spared us a glance as we found places in the back row. My eyes adjusted to the dimness and then I gasped. Bride and groom were standing before the minister, their backs turned towards the congregation. The woman was dressed in traditional Hanna costume. The minister had just blessed the couple and in a loud voice I heard him say, 'I now pronounce thee man and wife, and let no man pull thee asunder. Amen.'

There was an excited tittering among the congregation, and then the couple stiffly embraced, then turned and for the first time we saw their faces. The girl was not Rebecca, nor was the bridegroom the Childeater. I could hear Jason chuntering with disbelief. He whispered into my ear. 'There were two weddings . . . this must be the other one.'

In frustration, we waited as the newly wed couple passed down the aisle. While the remainder of the congregation flocked from the church, our enquiries bore fruit. This was indeed the second wedding of the day. The first, during the afternoon, had been between a member of another faith, Nate Kirby, and a Hanna girl, Rebecca van Bremer. The couple had left town immediately after the service.

ELEVEN

I guess my heart was in my boots as we left the church. We were perhaps closer to our quarry than we had been for some time, yet the Childeater had struck me a terrible blow in taking Rebecca for his wife. Jason was shaken too, but we both agreed that we must follow up the trail as soon as possible. Firstly, Jason had to acquire a fresh mount. We found the livery-stable was closed for the Sabbath. We were directed to an adjacent house where the hostler lived and after much persuasion and bartering, Jason purchased a chunky gelding. The time of day was against us; the sun and land surrounding the town were dissolving slowly into the mystery of twilight.

We queried townsfolk for any information about the first wedding, and where the couple were heading for when they left, but nobody knew anything. I asked a woman if the couple had had a child with them, but the response was a shake of the head. Also, the minister had left Salvation Bluffs on his journey homeward to Woodenshoe Gulch. He was truly an elusive man and had played an unsuspecting part in deepening this tangle of misery.

Despite the oncoming night, we quickly purchased some supplies and rode out of town, following the canyon trail into the mountains, hoping that somehow we might spot a camp-fire ahead of us that would prove to be that of the Childeater. But as darkness descended and we urged our horses along the deserted trail, nothing occurred to give us hope.

We camped in a hollow and set our horses to graze, started a small fire from dead willow branches and cooked our supper of beans, corned beef and eggs. We made coffee from puddle-water, scooping it up in a tin cup and allowing it to stand for a while to let the sediment settle. Later, we took to our blankets, our saddles for pillows, and I wondered what torment Rebecca was undergoing on this her wedding night. And what had happened to little Ella?

But at that moment Jason's thoughts were on less important matters. 'Did thou ever get any of that liniment for my pimples?'

'Sure I did,' I gasped. 'I clean forgot. I got it from Dr McConnell's. It's in my saddle-bag. I'll give it you in the morning.'

'Could do with it now, Frank.'

I grunted impatiently, but I sat up, opened up my saddle-bag, found the small bottle and passed it across to him. 'Rub it in three times a day.'

He muttered his thanks and immediately started rubbing the liniment into his jaw. 'I been thinking,' he said. 'I figure we are on the right track. We certainly didn't pass Childeater on the trail to Salvation Bluffs, so that most likely means he has pressed on in this direction. Other side of this mountain range is the town of Buffalo Hump. Could be they're heading that direction. There's a way station ahead of us in the mountains. He may have stopped there. We can certainly ask.'

I nodded, though my maudlin mood had not lifted.

I lay awake for a long while, listening to the sounds of the night – the drone of cicadas, the rush of nighthawks through the darkness, gulping bugs as they went. As always Rebecca's face loomed in my mind, trusting and honest, and at this moment I wondered if she was being violated at the hands of a man more beast than human.

We were astir at dawn, watching the rising sun set the cloud banks aflame. After eating a few crackers and thinking we'd get something more substantial at the way station, we pressed on along the trail, riding through canyons, with clumps of brush and scattered juniper marking the slopes on each side. Soon the sky was a searing blue, delicate, wind-whipped clouds fighting a losing battle to soften its severity. We strained our eyes, seeking any tracks that might indicate the Childeater's party, but found nothing beyond the footprints of wild creatures.

We reached the way station just before noon. It was a shabby place, that had outlived its chief use when the stage-line had stopped running. Now it served as a drinking hole and overnight stop for occasional travellers. We hitched our horses to the rail and stepped inside, blinking at the dimness after the brightness of the sun. The place stank of stale food and beer and other even less wholesome things. The half-dozen men who were slouched over the bar and tables glanced up at us, as if challenging our right to enter, staring at Jason in particular because of his old-world garb. One of them emitted a scornful snigger. Eventually they resumed their drinking and talking. We sidled up to the bar. My heart was bursting with questions, but I decided to play it cool. I ordered a beer and Jason drew a strange look from the barman when he asked for water. None the less our order was served.

Trying to appear nonchalant, I enquired if some friends of ours had passed through – a group with a Hanna woman and a little girl.

The barman was a surly, lazy-looking individual. He was running a greasy rag over his bar-top and didn't stop his slow wipe. He shook his head. 'Ain't been no strangers passing through for days.'

I grunted my disappointment. I was aware of the intense stare of a man sitting at a table in the corner of the room. A Mexican with a long mournful face. When I met his gaze he looked away.

'Strangers in this place stick out like a sore thumb,' the barman commented. 'We'd have spotted them for sure.'

We were hungry so we ordered some food and sat down at a table to await its arrival. When it was eventually served it was hardly worth the wait, but we were in no mood to complain. After we'd finished eating, I enquired where the privy was and was directed out the back. It was a three-holer in a flimsy shack with wide gaps in its frail walls. It looked as though a good blast of wind, either from inside or out, would blow it away. Having relieved myself, I was pulling up my jeans when I heard voices from outside. A couple were walking towards the house – a small girl talking to a woman, obviously her mother. I could see them through the gaps in the privy woodwork.

'Can I go and talk with her, Ma?' the girl enquired. 'Maybe she'd read me a story.'

'No, Jenny. She's got to stay hidden with Señor Jeronimo.'

'Why has she got to stay hidden?'

'Because she has. Don't ask any more questions.'

They continued talking, but they walked on and passed out of ear-shot.

I tried to bridle my excitement. What I'd heard might have no significance. On the other hand there were questions which needed answering. Who was the *she* and why did she have to remain hidden? And the Señor Jeronimo . . . was he the Mexican who had stared at me? Could Rebecca be a prisoner, here at this run-down place. Leaving the privy, my eyes dwelt on the upper storey. Tattered, filthy curtains were drawn across the two front windows. Wild hopes began to churn in me. I walked around the building and noticed that wooden steps led up to the upper storey on the outside. I recalled there were also steps leading up from the bar. I returned to the bar room, finding Jason dozing in his chair. I noticed that the Mexican had left his position in the corner.

I nudged Jason awake and whispered what I had heard, watching his eyes widen. We both gazed around. Nobody was paying us any attention.

'You take the outside stairs,' I whispered. 'I'll go up from here.'

He nodded, undid the hooks of his coat and loosened his six-shooter in its holster, after which he rose and walked calmly for the door, giving the barman a farewell wave of his hand. I waited a few seconds, then I stood up and moved towards the stairs.

'Where you goin', mister?' the barman called, sparking into life. 'Upstairs is private.'

'Just need to see Señor Jeronimo,' I responded.

The barman spluttered something, but I went up those stairs three at a time, drawing my gun. I reached a small landing off which one door led. Was I making some foolish mistake or could Rebecca be on the other side? I was in no mood for dallying.

I turned the handle, the door gave to my shove. Jeronimo was standing there, and I was fleetingly aware of little Ella's saucer-like eyes staring from behind him. As I registered what I was seeing, Jeronimo reacted, hurling something heavy directly at me. Before I could get out of the way, it struck me, some sort of ornament, causing me to double up as it fell shatteringly to the floor. With it went my gun, the shock of impact loosening my fingers from it. He sprang forward, grabbing me with his strong sinewy hands, driving me back on the landing. I tried to fend him off with my one good hand, but it was hopeless, and I could hear the barman coming up the stairs behind me. Jeronimo got a grip on my throat, started to squeeze. I tried to kick him free, but there was no room to swing my leg. At that moment, the gun went off with a deafening roar, and Jeronimo let out a grunt and relinquished his grip. He staggered against the banisters, splintered through them and fell downwards out of sight, landing with a thud which shook the place. I gazed at the barman's horrified face, but he wilted before my glare and backed down the stairs, then I swung back to see that Jason, his gun still drawn, had entered through the outside door of the room.

We both rushed to the white-faced Ella. She was tied to a bed, and was speechless with the horror of events. Jason drew a knife and slashed the rope securing her. I gathered her up, gave her a reassuring hug and murmured, 'You're safe now, honey.'

Meanwhile Jason had gone through the inner door of the room and down the stairs. I carried Ella and stood on the small landing, gazing down through the shattered railings. The barman was standing wringing his hands in dismay. Jeronimo was spread-eagled on the floor, blood staining his shirt, his mournful face twisted with pain. The rest of the bar's customers had vacated the premises, knocking chairs over in their haste to escape any bullets.

One glance satisfied me that Jeronimo was in no condition to do us any harm, and the barman wanted no more violence. I went down the stairs, listening to the Mexican's groaning. I lowered Ella to the ground and Jason and I stood over him. A bullet had taken him in the shoulder, coming out through the front, causing the blood to well out, but it was the fall which had done him the greatest injury.

'I theenk my back is broken,' he groaned, and I could see beads of sweat standing out on his brow.

Jason said, 'Thou were with Childeater? Thee burned our cabin, killed my father?'

The Mexican didn't answer in words, but his furtive eyes, gazing up at us from beneath bushy eyebrows, indicated an affirmative.

'Where's Childeater now?' I snapped out, 'And the Hanna woman?'

He closed his eyes, renewing his groaning. I lost my patience, showing him the same ruthlessness as he possessed. I hit him across the face with the back of my hand, causing an ugly red weal to flame on his cheek, having him crying out.

'Where are they?' I repeated.

'I cannot move,' he groaned. 'I need a doctor . . . I beg you.'

'Where are they!'

'Tell us,' Jason said, showing more patience than me, 'and I'll fetch a doctor for thee.'

He licked his lips, wincing with pain. His bloodshot eyes flicked over us, seeking mercy, finding little. I figured an undertaker might be of greater use to him than a doctor.

He was mumbling. 'The gang split up . . .'

'Where's Childeater and the woman?' I snarled again, filling my voice with all the malevolence I could muster.

He flinched, fearing that I was going to hit him again, half raising his hand to fend me off. Then suddenly he relented, 'His hideout at Buckthorn Valley. That's where he's taken her. He'll keel me for telling you.'

'Why were you holding the kid?' I demanded.

He sighed deeply. 'Childeater said I must keep her. If the woman, hees wife, misbehaved, I was to kill the child. But I wouldn't have done that. I swear to God, I wouldn't.'

I straightened up, took Ella's hand in mine. She'd been used as a pawn in this awful game.

'Buckthorn Valley,' I murmured. 'Where is it?'

'It is to the north,' Jason answered. 'Once, I went there.'

The Mexican groaned again. He didn't deserve much sympathy, but the sight of him, suffering as he was, was pitiful. If his back was broken, moving him would be tantamount to killing him.

'Can you draw me a rough map of the Buckthorn Valley country?' I asked Jason.

He shook his head. 'I do not know it well enough, Frank.'

I swung my attention back to the Mexican. His eyelids had dropped down but I roused him with a prod in the ribs. 'How do I find Childeater's hide-away?'

He hesitated, grimaced with pain, then said, 'Follow along the road to Yellowcat Crossing. Eet's maybe thirty miles . . . wild country. Cross the river, then take Fool's Trail, You'll find Childeater's cabin at the end of eet.'

'Fool's Trail?' I didn't like the sound of that.

'Yes, Fool's Trail,' the barman cut in. 'It was discovered by William Fool, way back in the 1840s.'

'*Si, señor*,' the Mexican groaned. 'There is a signpost, a wooden board. It's a short cut . . .' His voice gave out. He sure wasn't shamming his pain.

I debated whether this pair could be trusted. I decided I didn't have much option. I turned to Jason. 'You best take Ella back to Salvation Bluffs, lodge her somewhere safe until we can pick her up later on, then follow me up. Try and find Buckthorn Valley. At the same time you can get a doctor out here to attend to this devil.'

Jason pondered for a moment, figured he saw the sense in what I was proposing, even if I wasn't convinced myself, and nodded.

As we prepared to go our separate ways, the barman dosed Jeronimo with whiskey to relieve his pain. Ella gave me a big kiss and a hug before she departed. 'Bring Mama back,' she pleaded as we said our farewells, and I said I'd do my best and prayed that my best would be good enough.

I still didn't feel happy that Jeronimo was telling the truth. He could well be sending me off on a fruitless chase that would have me lost in wilderness, or worse. The only reassuring factor was that he seemed willing to do anything, even betray his former boss, provided it offered him some prospect of relieving the agony he was suffering.

TWELVE

Buckthorn Valley country was rugged. The trail ran parallel to the river, and on each bank were vivid colonies of sunflowers, as yellow as butter. Flocks of piñon jays and sparrows darted in front of me. I'd eaten all the provisions I had with me and was feeling hungry, but the need to travel with all possible haste prevented my stopping apart from brief pauses to rest my horse. I pressed on for hours. Jeronimo had mentioned thirty miles. It seemed more like a hundred. I wondered if I had somehow bypassed the crossing. But eventually I saw a rough board proclaiming 'Yellowcat Crossing' and here the river was fordable. There was some sort of slab of rock below the surface, forming a natural bridge, and as I urged the roan through the shallow water I didn't even get my legs wet. On the far side I spotted a fingerboard. It should have pointed to an adjacent opening in the cliff, but, being rotten, had dropped from its support and was lying face down. I slid from the roan's back and turned it over. It said:

FOOL'S TRAIL
VERY NARROW

I restored the sign to its rightful position, hammering the nail into the support with the butt of my six-gun. I figured the sign should be easily seen when, or if, Jason followed me up. I didn't like the way the 'very' was emphasised, but I remounted and heeled the roan forward. I wondered if William Fool had ever existed.

The trail was a kind of terrace, its entrance some fifteen feet wide. For maybe an hour the going was easy, but presently the terrace grew steeper, winding around a precipice. Jeronimo had said it was a short cut to where Childeater, and please God, Rebecca, were holed up. Poor Rebecca. How was she withstanding the ordeal?

The trail gradually tapered down to the narrowest of paths. After I'd progressed for a further half-hour, I was convinced I'd been duped. Loose pebbles squirted out from beneath the roan's hooves and disappeared over the rim, landing so far down that I heard no sound. Now the path diminished to merely two feet wide and I was obliged to dismount, intending to lead the horse. As I swung from the saddle, I glanced down and grunted with horror. Below me was a sheer drop of more than a hundred feet. For a second I just clung there, too scared to regain my place in the saddle lest I lose my grip altogether. I closed my eyes, let fear wash through me, felt the blood pounding in my temples. Heights had never been my strong point. I'd been nominated for balloon duty in Cuba to spy out on the enemy, but had declined when I learned the dizzy altitude to which those bags of air ascended. Now I knew full well why they called this path Fool's Trail. And in venturing along it, I'd been the biggest fool of all. I figured if William Fool had ever existed, he must've been some sort of fly.

Somehow I squirmed myself beneath the belly of the horse and restored my trembling frame to the path. Jeronimo must have intentionally directed me in this direction, knowing that the way was nigh impassable. I forced my eyes to gaze downward, shuddered, and wondered how many other fools had plunged to their deaths on the rocks below.

On one side were great, loose, overhanging rocks impossible to ascend and looking as if the slightest breath of wind would have them avalanching downward. On the other side, the precipice plunged away, and I didn't fancy tempting fate with another glance into those giddy depths. The thought made my breath quicken. I was sure that the Childeater would never have come this way, particularly with an unwilling bride.

And then the faintest of distant sound drew my attention, forcing me to stem my fears and look beyond the edge. In the far distance, across a wide canyon studded with upthrusting juniper, a long ribbon of dust was rising and it was clear a horseman was down there, racing his animal at desperate speed. He must have been a good mile away, too far to determine his identity and I was certainly in no position to fumble round and extract my binoculars from my saddle-bag. I watched until he disappeared, his presence doing nothing to lessen my uneasiness. I emitted a frustrated sigh and refocused my attention on my predicament.

I was not alone in my concerns. The roan was as spooked as I was, his eyes rolling white, his nostrils flaring with nervousness as he hyperventilated. He was obviously dead against proceeding further, but his barrel was nearly the same width as the path, and it would be impossible to turn him between the wall of rock and the outer rim. There could be no way back. Furthermore, one slip of his nervous hooves might well have us both plummeting to our deaths.

But then my thoughts swung to Rebecca, as they so often did, even in the most unlikely places. I told myself I hadn't come all this way to get beaten by some dizzy trail.

On my hands and knees between the tremulous legs of my horse, I glanced forward. Ahead, the path twisted to the right, disappearing around the rock wall. Gritting my teeth, I squeezed between the forelegs of the horse, feeling like a prisoner pushing through the bars of his cell. For a moment I feared the animal might panic and lose his footing, but coaxing him with a calmness I did not feel, I quieted him.

I crawled forward, stemming my dizziness, closely hugging the upper face, hoping, praying, that beyond the sharp curve, the terrace would widen. I reached the point where the path disappeared beyond the rock wall, inched my way onward, peered around – and exhaled with profound relief. My prayers had been answered. The path expanded to a width of some six feet and began to descend. Seldom was a sight more welcome.

But my troubles were not over. For a good half-hour I coaxed and cajoled the horse to step forward. I had the confidence of knowing that safety lay around the bend. He clearly wasn't prepared to take my word for it. With mule-like stubbornness, he planted his forelegs to the full width of the path and would not yield to my tugging his reins. I began to grow desperate. It would be unfair to shoot the beast for having fears similar to my own, yet it seemed downright wrong to leave him standing here. I moved back around the bluff and sat down, trying to think up a way of getting him mobile, but my brain seemed as dead as a plucked chicken. It seemed I didn't have much option but to leave him. I felt downright frustrated. It was growing dark now, making the situation even more bleak. Truly, I had never been in such a God-forsaken place, and as I crouched there all my troubles, all my doubts, seemed to gang up, swamping my mind with gloom. Events sometimes took my mind away from the throbbing pain in my arm, but it was always there, making me groan when I attempted to bring my right hand into play. Generally, now, I'd become quite adept with my left hand, but that didn't give me much satisfaction.

My depressing contemplations were suddenly interrupted by the clop of hooves and my equine friend moved around the bluff, nickering a greeting and acting as if he hadn't a care in the world. My dad had once told me that horses were as unpredictable as women. I guessed he was right.

The full moon, bright as a silver shield, swam into the heavens, casting down a brightness unhealthily close to daylight in some places, while elsewhere it plunged the sheltered nooks into evil blackness. It occurred to me, as I followed that crazy path downward, that I was clearly silhouetted against the cliff face. In the moonlight, anybody waiting below would be well aware of my approach. Maybe Childeater made a point of watching the path for the first sign of any unwelcome company. But for the moment, the only company the roan and I were afforded came from a great horned owl that, for reasons known only to itself, chose to follow us for much of the way, uttering its ghostly cries into the night.

It must have been close to midnight when my worst suspicions were proved correct. *The Mexican Jeronimo had directed me into the very jaws of a trap.*

THIRTEEN

Maybe I'd lapsed into complacency, knowing that I had no other option but to run the gauntlet on the downward slope of Fool's Trail. I wondered if I was getting close to Childeater's hideaway, or was I on a futile errand?

The contours of the land had changed about me, both the high wall to my right and the abyss to the left become less steep. To my front the upward gradient was cloaked with trees. The moon had now retired behind cloud, and in the resultant murkiness, my horse suddenly slipped on the loose shale and struggled to retain his footing.

It was at that moment that the shot blasted off, buckling the animal under me.

I had only a fraction of a second to kick free of the stirrups as I was thrown from the saddle. Helplessly, I was tumbled over the rim of the trail, the reverberation of the shot filling my ears. Now, thank God, I was not pitched into a yawning abyss but on to sloping slabs of granite broken up with mat-like tangles of spruce. But such details were for later reflection. I rolled downward and came to a jarring halt against the stump of a tree, yelling out as the breath was lambasted from my pain-racked body. More shots were splintering the rock about me, setting sharp fragments slicing the air.

I had hit the ground awkwardly, crushing my useless arm. I knew that my life was hanging by a thread; the next bullet could well have my name on it. I steadied my breath and forced myself to roll over, then half rising, stumbled to some low boulders and dropped down, conscious that more shots were blasting off, sounding like deadly firecrackers. I got my own gun from its holster and glanced around, seeking a target in the darkness but finding none. The gunfire appeared to have come from the wooded slope to my left. Somebody had clearly been waiting for me, but his marksmanship must have been hampered by the gloom and the fortuitous stumble of the horse had been enough to edge me from the sights of his rifle. Up on the path, I could hear the roan thrashing around, his breath rasping, but my view of him was obscured by the overhanging gradient. He'd taken a bullet and this grieved me, especially after the courageous way he'd conquered his fears to get me here.

I figured the best hope for my own survival was to shift my position quickly and get into the timbered slope across the other side of the trail. Then, in the darkness I might be able to come up with some sort of plan. I felt pretty certain my attacker, presumably Childeater, was operating alone. Even so, if it came to physical contact, I would be severely handicapped with one arm bandaged and inoperative. I determined to make a dash for the trees on the right. I got to my feet, ran zigzagging across slabs of broken granite, some of which see-sawed beneath my feet. I expected a shot at any moment. I was not disappointed.

The hateful crack of the gun came from closer than previously, and, simultaneously, I felt a sickening thump in my left side, just beneath the rib cage, and I was sent staggering forward; even so, I managed to avoid falling and stumbled on, crossing over the trail, to reach the trees. Once into their shadows, I dropped down.

Wondering how badly I was hit, I reached round. There was no blood, nor even pain in that particular spot. It must have been a lump of ricocheting rock or earth that had struck me rather than a bullet. I grunted with relief, knowing that any good fortune was of a temporary nature.

I was now crouching in a narrow fringe of timber. The trees, pale-trunked aspen, stood in serried formation, their leafy crowns rustling in the breeze. They would be further agitated by any movement I made.

Underfoot, the ground was twisted with tangled spruce growing over the rock. Dawn was now agitating the eastern sky, stabbing pale fingers of light across the slopes. Through the trees, I could see the ground rising, a jumble of loose slabs, towards a summit. I wished I had my rifle, but that was still in the scabbard on the horse. To attempt to reach it would be tantamount to suicide.

With despairing eyes, I combed the area to my front, and suddenly I saw him. This was Childeater without a doubt. I'd never come face to face with him before, but I'd gazed at his Wanted poster enough times. He was moving confidently down the opposite slope, loping through the low scrub like a shadowy wolf. Knowing that I would never hit him at this range with my six-shooter, I forced myself up and hurried through the trees, the ground rising beneath my feet as I went, causing the going to get even more hazardous. The racket of my own movement, the whisperings of quaking aspen, seemed deafening. Soon, the trees had thinned, little more than storm-blasted shrubs. I burst clear of them, clambered furiously across jagged granite, knowing that I was exposed. My boot caught on the ridged ground. I stumbled, fell, the gun clattering from my grasp. Pain stabbed through my ankle. For a moment I thought it was broken or badly sprained. I climbed up, put my weight on it and realized it would still support me. In desperation, I fumbled around and recovered the weapon. I struggled to stem the rasp of my breathing, feeling like a hunted animal. For a moment I heard nothing, then suddenly came the swishing of foliage in the aspens behind me. I tensed, lifting my revolver. To my surprise, a bighorn sheep, an old ram, burst clumsily from the trees, stood sniffing the air before moving back into obscurity.

I pushed on, the gradient becoming even more acute. Ahead of me, I glimpsed a summit, and I imagined that once I reached it I might be in a more commanding position. Again I paused and this time I heard the unmistakable sound of somebody coming through the trees behind me. I cursed, but determined to try for the summit. If I could get him on open ground, I might stand a chance of felling him with my hand-gun.

But first I had to cross that open ground myself. Gritting my teeth, I lunged upward, came clear of sheltering foliage and realized that the crest was about twenty yards ahead of me. I'd practically crossed the intervening distance, when the gun sounded again, and this time a crippling pain slammed into my upper left thigh, leaving me in no doubt that I'd been hit by a bullet. I hit the ground, the pistol knocked from my grasp. Already blood was soaking my trouser leg. I was sprawled face down, stunned, when I heard his low laugh from behind me. 'Pinkerton man!' he hissed. 'So you figured I didn't know you was following me. I've waited for this moment for days. And now, my friend, you are going to suffer. You're going to die slowly, just like you deserve.'

I tried to collect my senses. Gingerly, I rolled over, sitting up. For the first time I got a good look at Childeater Hawkes. He was not a tall man, but squat and thick-set, with a neck which seemed as wide as his head. His darkly bearded, swarthy face had haunted my nightmares. Now those nightmares had become awesome reality. He was clad in an old coat, and he was holding a double-barrelled rifle lined up with my head. He laughed again, revealing his uneven teeth.

'Where's Rebecca?' I demanded.

His grin widened. '*Mrs Hawkes* to you!' he snarled. 'She's a happily married woman and she wants nothing to do with trash like you.'

The words were hardly out of his mouth when a rustling sounded in the aspens downslope, and I saw his eyes waver sideways. Then he turned his head slightly. He was turning back, muttering, 'Only that damned sheep!' when I lunged out and grabbed his ankle. He kicked my hand away, laughing scornfully, at the same time swinging the barrel of his rifle in an ark. He caught me a vicious blow across my left forearm, stepping back.

I was slumped over, unashamedly sobbing with the punishment I'd taken. I was completely at this man's mercy.

'None of your tricks, Pinkerton man.' He was leering at me, his lupine features stark in the early light. He lowered his voice, his threat coming with chilling intensity. 'I've shot you in the right leg, so the left leg will be next. I wonder how many bullets you can take before you peg out.'

He was aligning his gun with my leg, flexing his finger on the trigger, toying with me like a cat with a mouse. The grin of the devil on his face ... and then a woman's shriek sounded from behind him. 'Stop it!'

I raised my head and saw Rebecca, bedraggled and white-faced, scrambling up the slope.

'Get away, woman!' he snarled, but she didn't heed him and rushed on, grabbing hold of the gun, forcing it upward. He reacted with brute force, cursing her to high heaven. He jerked the butt of his rifle into her face, slamming her away from him.

Now I acted with instinct beyond desperation, determined to fight to the death if it had to be, somehow finding strength I didn't know existed. I went crazy, clawed on to his collar, kicking him despite the agony in my leg. Amazingly, I caught him off balance, head-butting him, ramming my elbow into his guts. Even so he staggered back, would have retaliated without a doubt, but Rebecca appeared to rear up from nowhere, hurling herself against his back. One moment he was there, the next he was gone and Rebecca's scream was ringing in my ears. I hobbled in his wake, realizing that he had stumbled over the rim. I hadn't realized that the summit was a sheer drop on the far side. Rebecca was at my side as we gazed down. It was a deep drop into a canyon. No man could survive such a fall, or so we thought.

Rebecca was all at once in my arms, clinging tightly, sobs racking her body. And then her words came. 'Ella . . . he said that if anything bad happened to him, or I tried to escape, she would die . . .'

'Don't worry,' I reassured her. Ella's safe. Jason's taken her back to Salvation Bluffs.'

'Thank God,' she cried, some of the tension easing out of her. 'My prayers have been answered.'

'How did you find us here?' I asked. 'You saved my life.'

'He brought me to a cabin near here. But this evening a man from the way station came. I did not hear what he said but he must have told Childeater that thou were coming along the Fool's Trail. Childeater went out to watch for thee. I guessed what was happening, but I was almost too late. I heard the shot and followed up.'

I nodded. I recalled the horseman I'd seen. It must have been the way station barman. The route he had taken had been the shorter way to the hideaway cabin, not the way I'd been sent.

'Did you know I was following you?' I asked.

'I prayed that thou were.'

But despite what had happened, all was not well with Rebecca. She'd taken a nasty blow across the side of her face and blood was trickling down. But something else was troubling her.

'I have sinned,' she sobbed. 'A Hanna woman should never commit violence, but I pushed him over the edge. I . . .'

'You had no alternative,' I murmured. 'You saved my life. He deserved nothing better.'

She nodded, not entirely convinced, but gradually her doubts gave way to relief and we were clinging to each other. But then a sound intruded – an animal-like groan of pain coming from beyond the summit edge. In horror we slipped from each other's arms and again gazed into the abyss. The drop-off was acute, its rough surface cracked and eroded by the elements. For the first time we saw the narrow ledge half-way down, a ledge choked with ferns and other growth, enough for a man to cling to and there, sprawled on his back was Childeater Hawkes, writhing with pain, his eyes gazing up at us. Even if he had been uninjured, there was no way he could escape his narrow refuge without the aid of a rope. Sickened, I glanced around and noticed that he had dropped his rifle before stumbling over the edge. I stooped and gathered it up. Here was the very weapon that a few minutes earlier had been used to bring me down. I checked the mechanism. There were shells in the breech. 'I can shoot him,' I said. 'Put him out of his suffering.'

Rebecca gazed at me, her eyes wide, but her lips formed no utterance to discourage me.

I pointed the barrel downwards, lined up the sights. Childeater gazed up at me, defiance momentarily replacing the pain in his face.

'Kill me, Pinkerton man,' he shrieked out. 'You killed her last husband. Now kill me . . . and then she'll be all yours! She's nothing but a hell-cat anyway!'

His words sank into my brain. He was Rebecca's husband. One shot would rid us of him, and, if Rebecca would have me, I would marry her myself. There was nothing I wanted more. But I couldn't do it. I let the rifle slide to the ground. I would not commit cold-blooded murder, nor would I afford him the satisfaction of a bullet.

I knew that sooner or later Jason would turn up with the law. Hawkes could wait until somebody threw him down a rope. After that he would go on trial and in due course, hopefully, make the acquaintance of another rope – a judicial one.

My thigh was burning with pain and I could feel blood coursing down my leg, and yet again I was going to require the assistance of this wonderful woman at my side.

Leaving Hawkes to suffer on his narrow ledge, Rebecca helped me down that awful slope. It would forever be branded in my memory, along with the nightmare of what had happened here. We went through the trees and across a valley to where Childeater's ramshackle hideout was located. Once in the cabin, Rebecca set about making me as comfortable as possible, stemming the flow of blood. The bullet was still lodged in my thigh and I reckoned that a doctor would have to dig it out. I tried to make light of it, but I knew I was in a bad way. Afterwards, I bathed the blood away from her face, but she was more concerned about my welfare than her own. 'Thy body has taken too much suffering, Frank. A human being can only stand so much.'

That night, I did not sleep. The pain was too great. My leg stiffened, but next morning I gritted my teeth and forced myself to move. Rebecca accompanied me up on to the path, helping me as I hobbled along. My thigh-bone felt as if it was broken, the edges were grating against each other. She had found an old broom for me to use as a crutch. The sun had lifted and the rocks and trees rippled behind a veil of heat. I wondered if Childeater was still alive, or had he succumbed to the elements and his injuries? Maybe even now the buzzards were pecking at his remains.

To my satisfaction, I discovered that the roan had righted himself and had found some grass to graze on. I called to him but he wouldn't come. He, like me, had taken a bullet wound. I could see a red-grooved slash across the flank but it was clear he'd survive. As Rebecca and I turned away, he started to follow. He knew where his bread was buttered.

I did not yearn to see whether Childeater survived or not. The mere thought of casting my gaze upon him seemed abhorrent. I'd let him stew in own his juices for a while, if he had any left. But above the summit I saw buzzards circling.

Rebecca and I kept watch from a bluff on the west side of the cabin, sitting together in the shade of a lone juniper. We had a grand view of the surrounding terrain, of the twisting mountain path and of the gullies and fissures that stretched away into the distance. She was very quiet and I knew what she had experienced lay heavily upon her. And now I knew I must increase her burden. I had to be honest with her, just as I had with Jason.

'Rebecca, it was me who shot Kasper. I had to do it to save a man's life. Kasper was taking aim at Sheriff Ollerton.

She acknowledged it with a curt nod, almost matter-of-fact. 'I know thou killed him. I heard what Childeater shouted out. Thou were doing thy job. Kasper paid for his sins.'

I breathed in sharply. 'I'm sorry. I should have told you before. It's easy to kill somebody. It's not easy to live with it afterwards.'

'It is in the past. We can change nothing.'

'Thank you, Rebecca,' I whispered. 'I love you.'

She reached out and rested her hand on mine in acknowledgement of my words. Later, when we returned to the cabin she sat in a chair and when she looked up, her eyes were glistening with tears, and I sensed that she was not crying for me, but for the sadness of her life, and I did not intrude.

Next day we saw riders approaching, led by an unmistakable figure in Hanna black. Jason had not let us down. I fired into the air, attracting his attention and within twenty minutes, he, the sheriff from Salvation Bluffs and his four men reached the cabin. They had not taken the Fool's Trail but had used the shorter and far safer route. In answer to Rebecca's frantic questioning, Jason confirmed that Ella was safe and being cared for by a Salvation Bluffs family. He listened, with astounded eyes, as we explained our own experiences. After that, we all climbed to the summit, Jason helping me along. I was apprehensive at the thought of what we might find. Perhaps Childeater had disappeared, somehow squirmed from our grasp in an incredible escape, intent on exacting yet further revenge. Or maybe all that remained of him was a heap of buzzard-picked bones. But as we gazed over the rim, he was still there. He was asleep or unconscious, but he roused himself at the sound of our voices. A rope was thrown down and he was hauled up from his ledge. His leg was twisted awkwardly, but his face was an even worse sight, for it smouldered with black hatred. And that hatred was directed at me. No words were needed to express it. He was weak from hunger and thirst, and supped greedily from a canteen, then he was tied up, being shown the complete lack of compassion he deserved. That same afternoon we started back towards Salvation Bluffs.

The thought that this evil man was still Rebecca's husband sickened me. I knew that divorce was strictly abhorrent to the Hanna faith, but I felt sure that justice would be done and relieve the world, and in particular Rebecca, of this awful man.

Unfortunately, I was to be proved wrong.

FOURTEEN

As Rebecca had said, my physical shape was pretty bad. After the capture of Zackery Hawkes, I was taken to hospital, and my father had his physician friend, Edwin Jakes, assess my condition. He immediately had me transferred to a hospital in New York and oversaw my treatment personally, a colleague of his carrying out the actual surgery. Jakes told me that the bullet was embedded so deeply in my thigh that it would be impossible to extract. He doubted that I would ever be able to walk without a stick. As for my hand: he confirmed that Dr O'Connell's prognosis had been correct. Even so, I was very fortunate. I had the best treatment available, although I prefer not to dwell on the details of it, and all my medical bills were met by the Pinkerton Agency. Afterwards, I embarked upon my recuperation in good spirits, the prospect of a better future beckoning me. However, news came through that set me back.

I knew that Hawkes had stood trial while I was undergoing treatment and I anticipated that the verdict and the severest sentence were just a formality. He'd surely sinned enough against innocent folk to deserve the gallows. In addition, Rebecca had been subjected to the most unspeakable physical and mental abuse. But his defence attorney was masterful and exploited some loophole in the law. The end result was that the judge showed leniency and sentenced Hawkes not to death but to twenty years in the penitentiary. I felt gutted. Wicked as it may seem, I'd been counting on the man's death and had anticipated that soon thereafter, I would ask Rebecca to be my wife, but now it appeared she was linked to him until either she or he died, barred from divorce by her religious beliefs.

I was convalescing, sitting in a wheelchair on the hospital lawn, when she came to visit me, having travelled by rail from Utah. It was wonderful to see her, to feel the warmth and the compassion that dwelt in her eyes. Despite her circumstances and all she had suffered, she looked radiant and she was excited by all the sights she was seeing, never having travelled far before. She told me that she and Ella had taken up temporary residence with a friend in Blessedville, which was God's Navel to everybody else. Jason was well and was soon to marry his Hanna girlfriend.

I leaned back, enjoying the sound of her gentle voice. We drank orange juice and ate dainty little sandwiches that the sister made for us. But time sped by and with Rebecca's departure growing nearer, depression descended upon me. It just wasn't fair that this vibrant, beautiful woman should be chained to a criminal like Hawkes. My gloom must have shown on my face for she asked me what was wrong.

'I covet another man's wife,' I said. 'Her name is Rebecca.'

She rested her hand on mine. 'Speak thy mind, Frank.'

'I love you. I guess I always have, right from the first time I awakened and gazed into your face. You've filled my mind ever since. I was going to ask you to marry me, but now, with Zackery Hawkes serving out his life sentence, everything's ruined. Rebecca, why don't you divorce him?'

'Oh Frank, I truly wish to be thy wife, but I cannot divorce him.' She paused for a moment, then added, 'But there is a way?'

'A way? What way?' My pulse had quickened.

'You do not know our faith very well.'

'I know that you do not believe in divorce.'

Her lips widened into a faint, secretive smile. 'The Hanna faith allows plural marriages.'

I swallowed hard. 'You mean a man can have more than one wife?' I wondered what she was getting at.

She nodded. 'And,' she said coyly, 'a woman can have more than one husband.'

I almost sprang from my wheelchair with joy.

'Yes, Frank McGarry,' she said. 'I will marry thee, if thou will have me.'

Six weeks later, I was discharged from hospital. I travelled overnight, enjoying the comfort of a Pullman coach before I was obliged to change. I arrived at God's Navel the following morning and soon found the house where Rebecca and Ella were lodging. Rebecca was sitting in the kitchen, labelling jars of fruit. I noticed that her eyes were red. She rose and was immediately in my arms. After we had kissed, she sliced me a generous portion of cherry pie and poured me a glass of milk, then we sat down. Although she was doing her utmost to show me a cheerful face, I could see that something was preying on her mind. To my astonishment, she stopped talking in the middle of our conversation, lifted her apron to her face and burst into tears.

I hugged her, trying to console her. 'What's wrong honey?'

'Frank,' she sobbed. 'I am with child. *His* child!'

The breath caught in my throat. 'You're sure? These things can sometimes . . .'

'Frank . . . I am sure!'

For a moment her sobbing continued. I drew out my handkerchief and she raised her face and I dried her eyes. I hated to see her so sad.

'Thou cannot marry me now, Frank. It would not be fair.'

'With me a crippled man, it was never fair,' I countered 'but that wasn't going to stop us.'

'It is not that,' she gasped, impatience showing in her voice. 'How could thee marry a woman who has borne *his* offspring. It will be wicked, like him . . .'

'It'll make no difference,' I said. 'It's you I love. We'll overcome our problems. Besides, children do not always resemble their father.'

She didn't answer.

'We'll build our future together,' I persisted, 'no matter how difficult it is. We'll face things together. We've been through too much already to be beaten by Zackery Hawkes.'

So I thought.

We were married a month later in the Hanna Church at Woodenshoe Gulch, Jason standing as groom's man. Soon Rebecca was immensely pregnant and I knew that her fears were the same as mine, though we never spoke of it: was she carrying a monstrous giant of a child who would follow in his father's footsteps? The weeks sped by, the child was late in arriving, and eventually the birth was very difficult. Rebecca had to have her belly slit open, just as the mother of Julius Caesar had, so that the child could be lifted out, otherwise both mother and baby would have died. Thus Zackery Hawkes' child was delivered into the world. Rebecca and I breathed a thankful sigh of relief it was not a boy but a girl. She was not a monster nor was she evil. Indeed, Elizabeth Mary was the sweetest child imaginable, and she took the name of McGarry and I brought her up, and loved her, as my own.

I was retired from the Pinkerton Agency and in the following years, we set up home in God's Navel and watched Elizabeth Mary grow. We ensured that she had a truly loving upbringing and, when the time came, a good education. We never told her about her parenthood. Looking back, I guess this was wrong, but we thought it was right at the time.

I was proud too of Ella. She matured to womanhood so quickly. She married a good farming man and set up her own home.

As for Rebecca and me, we lived as happily as we could, and she gave me a son, Robert, and he attended college and later returned and was baptized into the Hanna faith as was the custom.

Rebecca was the beacon of my life and our love grew year by year, and we tried to put the past behind us, although at the back of my mind was always the harrowing thought that as well as being my wife, she was also wedded to Zackery Hawkes.

But I gleaned strength, even some peace of mind, after I too was baptized. I soon realized that the Hanna way was the only true way, and the customs that at first seemed strange – the old fashioned dress, the different practices of worship, the abstinence from alcohol and cursing, the disdain of embellishment – became acceptable as I saw the reasons behind everything.

After my father died, Rebecca and I moved to the family farmhouse in Kentucky. The land proved bountiful and we prospered.

In 1914, the Great War flared in Europe, and when our own country entered the conflict, I was prevented from enlisting by my disablement – that, and the religious beliefs that had now become my way of living.

A year after the armistice, I became an elder in the church and by now had learned the Pennsylvania Dutch tongue.

Elizabeth Mary had all her mother's beauty.

When she was eighteen, she was preparing to be baptized into the faith. But a week before the scheduled ducking ceremony, I was sitting at my desk preparing a sermon when she came to me with a startling question.

'Was I conceived out of wedlock, father?'

I was taken aback. I thought for a moment. 'No,' I said truthfully, thou were not.'

She looked mystified, but she nodded and went to her room.

During the next few days, she changed, withdrawing into herself and looking utterly miserable. Eventually she told us that she had discovered the truth, that I was not her true father. Furthermore, she no longer wished to live under the same roof as me; she wanted to go and lodge with her aunt in Salvation Bluffs. Neither Rebecca nor I ever found out how she had learned of her true parenthood. We could only imagine that she got sight of some document which started her probing into dates and other matters. But it was a sad blow, and one, thinking back, that we brought upon ourselves. We could do nothing to make her change her mind. She was determined to move in with her aunt – and we were obliged to let her go, hoping that she would come home soon. But she did not, despite numerous visits from her mother to try and persuade her. It left us heartbroken. Later on we heard that Elizabeth Mary and her aunt had moved to Baltimore in Maryland and our correspondence grew infrequent.

And always the shadow of Zackery Hawkes hovered over me, and I wondered what thoughts, what bitterness, were fermenting in his head as he endured the years behind bars.

Now his time was done. I read in the newspaper that he had been released from the penitentiary, and a sense of foreboding filled me. Would he travel to some faraway place, perhaps abroad, and start a new life, a reformed man, or would he seek Rebecca out and claim his marital rights? Maybe he even knew he had fathered a child.

It was cool October, 1923, but the sun was shining brightly. After Rebecca and I had enjoyed our midday meal, we sat at our oak table and gazed at some views through my stereoscope, magnificent views of the Arches country, laughing as we recalled happy memories, frowning as we recalled events that were not so pleasant. When she was busy clearing away the dishes, I sat on the porch in an old rocking-chair and lit up my pipe, remembering how Dad and I had sat in the same place all those years ago. So much had happened since then. I'd never anticipated being crippled for life, but at least I could now get around without a stick. And next year, subject to being elected, I would be a bishop in the Hanna faith and I was looking forward to that commitment wholeheartedly.

Through the banister of the porch, I spotted a lone horseman coming up the track towards the farmhouse – a dark, slow-moving figure. My pipe slipped from my mouth and I caught it, burning my fingers. I knew instinctively that it was the Childeater.

I came to my feet, pushing the rocker back, wishing that I had a gun. But at this moment I had nothing to defend myself with apart from the Bible I'd been studying and a hastily murmured prayer. I stood on the porch, feeling the blood drain from my face, my limbs weakening as if they were hollow. I watched man and horse get gradually nearer, and at last I could distinguish his gaunt features. The years had weathered him. There was a decided stoop to his shoulders. He wore a long black coat, and there was no way of telling whether or not he was carrying a gun. Even so, I sensed pending violence, and I was thankful that Rebecca was back in the kitchen, unaware that the man who had forced her into matrimony and planted his seed in her was here.

FIFTEEN

Zackery Hawkes reined his big sorrel horse as he reached the porch, and I guess he now saw me for the first time as I stood in the shadows. His face, hauntingly familiar, was lined with the passing years, but suddenly to my amazement, his mouth cracked into a smile. 'Frank Glengarry, my oh my, you don't look a day older than twenty years ago.'

He slid from the saddle, and reached out to shake my hand. For a second I left his hand hanging.

'I guess we have a lot in common, you and l,' he said, 'having married the same sweet woman.' He removed his hat revealing his close-cropped head. 'I done plenty o' thinking since I been in prison, and I realized how wicked I'd been. But I paid the penalty, and now I want to start a new and God-fearing life. Shake my hand, Frank. You and I must not be resentful to each other. I come here to say sorry for past wrongs, to let bygones be bygones.'

I hesitated, seeing his pale hand poised in front of me.

'Let bygones be bygones,' he repeated. 'After we've made our peace, and I've seen my pretty little wife and asked her forgiveness, I'll be on my way and I'll never cross your path again, Frank.'

What darned game was he playing at? I could do nothing else but take his hand and shake, and at that moment, to my dismay, Rebecca stepped from the house on to the porch. She was saying something, but the sight of our visitor had the words dying in her throat and her face glazed over with an look of horror.

Hawkes laughed. 'You gone as pale as a sheet, Rebecca, but there ain't no cause.' He turned back, unfastened his saddle-bag and drew out a Holy Bible. 'I live by this now,' he proclaimed, shaking it in the air. 'I've seen the light and the good Lord has showed me the path I should take. With you and Frank having lived as man and wife all these years, it would be sinful if I came back and imposed myself upon you. Like I told Frank, I've paid for my sins and all I want now is to see you again, maybe have a bite to eat, discuss a certain matter with Frank, then I'll be on my way.'

The harshness in Rebecca's eyes softened, but her words lacked conviction. 'If the Lord has brought thee here to make peace, if what thou say is true, then thou will not find us inhospitable.' I knew her head and all she believed in was overruling her gut feeling.

'God bless you both,' Hawkes said. 'Sure is a nice homely place you got here. The sort of home I've missed all these years.' A moment later he had stepped inside, still clutching his Bible, and was seated at our table while Rebecca served him some shoofly pie and a glass of milk. He placed his hat beside him and guzzled at the milk, the cream clinging to his moustache.

He put his glass down, belched, then said, 'Rebecca, I am here to ask your forgiveness for what I did to you. I am truly sorry.'

Rebecca hesitated. She sat at the table, her eyes averted, saying nothing, but I could see the tremor in her fingers.

'I am asking for your forgiveness,' Hawkes repeated.

Suddenly she raised her head. All the years of worshipping the Lord had given her true compassion, even for the worst of sinners. 'I forgive thee, Zackery Hawkes.' In a quieter tone she added, 'And I pray thou will forgive me for pushing thee over that cliff.'

He threw back his prison-shaved head, emitted a hearty laugh. 'Glory be to God!' he exclaimed. 'Oh, I've longed to hear those sweet words.' His eyes dwelt on Rebecca, and he was smiling. 'How does it feel, my little sweetheart, to have your two husbands sitting round the table, the best of friends after all those bad things that happened?'

Rebecca opened her mouth but no words emerged. I guessed she didn't know what to say.

'Are thou truly a follower of the Lord now?' I asked. I sensed a slyness in him, despite his gushing manner. I felt queasy.

He took a bite from his pie, speaking with his mouth full. 'I am . . . and I would dearly love to join the Hanna faith. Maybe we could talk that over.'

'Zackery Hawkes,' Rebecca cut in, 'did thou really eat two children when thee got snowed up in the mountains?'

He laughed again. 'That was just a story, my dear. Not even old Zackery was that bad.'

And so he talked on, explain how he'd been visited by an angel, there in the prison, and how the angel had convinced him of his evil ways and offered him a way of redemption. 'I sure grasped the chance with open hands,' he explained, 'swore I'd never step from the righteous path again. I've read the Bible from cover to cover and realized what I must do when they set me free. But it's been hard, real hard, spending all that time caged up. Plenty of time to think, for sure. Without my faith, I guess I wouldn't have stood it.'

'So thou art honestly repentant,' Rebecca said, 'and thou will go thy way and never come here again?'

Hawkes placed his gnarled hand on his Bible. 'I swear it before God. Frank and Rebecca, my friends, I am truly grateful for your forgiveness.'

'We forgive thee, Zackery Hawkes,' Rebecca repeated, trying to convince herself as much as him. 'Yes, we do.'

Hawkes assumed an expression of profound contentment. He put his hat on and stood up. 'I do thank you for your hospitality. Now I must be on my way.' He hesitated, then turned to me. 'There was just one other thing, Frank. I wonder if you and I could have a quiet word ... in private, maybe outside?'

My tenseness increased. I could feel my stomach churning over. I didn't trust him.

'Frank and I have no secrets from each other,' Rebecca said. 'Whatever needs to be said can be said in here.'

Hawkes shook his head. ' 'Tis man's talk,' he explained. 'Won't take a minute. Best if we just step outside.'

I exchanged a worried glance with Rebecca, but I nodded. 'It's cold now. I'll get my coat.'

I stepped across the hallway and entered the bedroom. I took my black coat down from its peg and put it on, fastening its hooks and eyes, then I crossed to the chest-of-drawers and slid open the top drawer. Inside, beneath some laundered shirts, was my old Colt revolver, loaded and ready, despite the fact that I had not fired it in anger for twenty years. I rested my hand upon it, but suddenly doubts clouded my mind. I was an elder of the church, perhaps I'd be a bishop next year. What right had I to doubt this man's plea of repentance?

I whispered a quick prayer, seeking the Lord's guidance.

I returned to the main room. I wondered what was so important that it couldn't be discussed within Rebecca's hearing.

Hawkes was smiling. 'I've never felt happier,' he said, 'knowing that you folks don't harbour no hatred for me now.'

Rebecca didn't respond, but she gave a slight nod and her face was taut.

'I'll be back soon,' I told her.

Hawkes' smile widened and he doffed his hat and again expressed his gratitude. We were about to go outside, when Rebecca spoke my name. I moved across to her and she kissed my cheek, then into my ear she whispered, 'Be careful, Frank. Please be careful.'

I nodded, gave her a hug, feeling the trembling in her body. When I rejoined Hawkes, I noticed he'd left his Bible upon the table.

He and I went outside and stepped down from the porch and crossed the yard, a chicken scampering before us. The wind was getting up and dark, heavy clouds were forming. 'Storm brewing,' I said.

'Sure is,' he responded.

As we walked, a couple of black crows lifted from the roof of the barn, the flap of their wings sounding bleakly loud.

'If I join your church,' Hawkes said as we moved around the side of the barn, 'will I have to grow a beard like yours and shave off my moustache.'

'That's our custom,' I said.

He glanced at the white markings on the side of the barn. 'What do them signs mean?'

'We believe they ward off evil spirits.'

He nodded his understanding. 'And do they?'

'There have been no evil spirits in this home up to . . . now.'

He laughed.

We had moved around the side of the barn, were out of view from the house. Here we stopped, facing each other. He made a strange sound in his throat, a suppressed mirthless chuckle. He unbuttoned his coat, allowed it to hang open, revealing the gun-belt around his waist. I stood with my hands plunged into the pockets of my own coat.

'I wanted to tell you something, Frank,' he said. 'It was not fitting for Rebecca's ears. You recall that gunfight in the Uinta Mountains, when you trapped us in that cave?'

'I do,' I said.

'Well, only three of us got away. Me, a fella called Clayton. And the third was a young girl called Mary Stafford.'

'A girl?' I gasped.

He nodded. 'I was going to marry her. She was carrying my child. But the shock of all that shooting was too much for her. She miscarried and she died a week later, bled to death.'

'I'm sorry,' I said. I remembered the pretty, straw-haired girl, obviously pregnant, who had collected Hawkes' mail, and the way I had trailed her to the cave. I felt bad at what he had said, but then a thought occurred to me. 'Maybe the folks in the banks and trains thou robbed suffered in similar ways. Maybe some of them had heart attacks with the shock of what thou did. That must've left their loved ones really sick.'

'Sure, I thought of that,' he said. 'But there's one big difference between what I did and what you did.'

'How come?'

'I've paid the penalty for what I done. You haven't . . . not until this moment!'

'I've been crippled by the bullet thou put into me, Zackery Hawkes,' I said. 'Thou killed old Frederik van Bremer, a man who had been kind to me, thou killed my horse, thou altered the whole course of my life.'

'That's not enough, Pinkerton man, not enough.' And now the sham sweetness was long gone from his evil face and I knew what his game was. For a fleeting second I noticed the sclera of his right eye, a permanent blood spot against the white, now fully displayed as he widened his eyes with anger. The old story hovered in my mind: once you saw that spot you were as good as dead.

With sickening inevitability, his hand slipped over the walnut butt of his six-shooter, his index finger embracing the trigger. He drew the weapon from its leather, held it barrel down.

'You've made it easy for me,' he said, 'being unarmed.'

'The Lord has guided me,' I said.

He lifted the gun.

I sprang for my life, plunging to the side as the weapon blasted off, I felt the jolting impact of a bullet at the same time as I hit the ground. Through the cloth of my coat, I fired left-handed, seeing his truculence replaced by amazement as lead ripped into his chest. He was thrown against the side of the barn, then he slumped down and flopped face forward into the dirt, blood showing the passage of his descent on the barn's hex-marked boards. I levered myself up, the blast of gunfire still ringing in my ears. I would've put another bullet into him if he'd stirred, but he didn't and gazing closer, I could see where the lead had emerged from his back. I guessed he'd been shot clean through the heart. I hoped so. I extracted my gun from my coat pocket and threw it down beside his corpse. I prayed I would never have cause to press another trigger.

My wrist was paining me. I heard Rebecca's alarmed call and she came running around the side of the barn, her shocked eyes taking in Hawkes' body.

'He tried to kill me.' I said.

'Oh Lord!' she cried, and then she noticed the way I was hunched over. 'Thou art hit.'

I nodded and examined myself. 'Shot my fingers clear off. Gave my wrist a nasty tug.'

'Frank . . .'

'Good job it was my false hand.'

I laughed. It was a crazy, relieved laugh. I had no right to laugh because a man had died, but I guess I felt light-headed. Rebecca didn't laugh. She was trembling like an aspen leaf, hugging on to me, her tears warm and salty as I kissed her. Afterwards, we went back into the house, knelt down and, with every ounce of sincerity in our hearts, thanked the good Lord for our salvation.